D1497983

ONE LAST GOOD-BYE

ONE LAST GOOD-BYE

•

Joyce and Jim Lavene

AVALON BOOKS
NEW YORK

PRINTED IN THE UNITED STATES OF AMERICA
ON ACID-FREE PAPER
BY HADDON CRAFTSMEN, BLOOMSBURG, PENNSYLVANIA

For our daughter, Jeni.
We are so proud of you!

Prologue

Palmer Mountain Gazette
March 15, 1944

*Tragedy struck today when a plane crashed into Pal-
mer Lake. Witnesses said the United States Navy plane
was flying low over the lake. The plane's wings dipped
and a loud backfire was heard from the engine. The
plane crashed into the lake, apparently killing both
men inside. Captain William Bost was the pilot. He is
the son of James and Myra Bost. His body, and that
of the copilot, have not been recovered.*

Chapter One

She was almost asleep. The faint breeze whispered through the pines, bringing with it the scent of the trees and the lake. An owl cried from somewhere in the darkness. Crickets and frogs sang their lullabies in tune to a peculiar whirring coming from the area of Diamond Mountain Lake, 1,500 feet straight down.

Night sounds and not much else. It was exactly what her fractured nerves needed.

Her body was exhausted after the hard day hiking the mountain trails through the Uwharries, but it had been a good day of long thoughts and sunshine. Another day stretched before her like an empty canvas, waiting to be filled with glimpses of sapphire-blue lakes and pink granite rock faces.

All of that, along with sunrise from the top of the mountain. No phones. No problems. Who could ask for anything more?

Her eyes had fluttered closed just as the peculiar

whirring in the distance turned into a loud rumble. A helicopter swooped up close to the side of the mountaintop. The long blades created a whirlwind that scattered her camp across the top and sides of the mountain. She made a dive for her backpack but it was gone before her fingers could reach the straps. A bright spotlight picked her out in the darkness.

"Sheriff Sharyn Howard. This is Deputy Joe Landers. Prepare for the vehicle to land!"

Sharyn put her hands over her ears. Between the close proximity of the helicopter itself and the blare from the loudspeaker, she was afraid her eardrums would burst.

The helicopter set down a few hundred yards from where she sat on the ground, still tangled in her sleeping bag and her tent. The door to the helicopter opened and a slight figure scooted out under the blades toward her.

"Sorry, Sheriff," Ernie apologized. "Joe doesn't have a brain in his head."

"What are you doing up here?" she asked, irritated.

"There's a situation in town, ma'am. We need you down there."

"It better be a triple-vampire homicide," she growled, trying to kick free from her sleeping bag and the collapsed tent.

Ernie started cleaning up the rest of her camping gear. "You know I wouldn't come up here and disturb your vacation for anything else, Sheriff."

"Sheriff Sharyn Howard." Joe's voice boomed out again. "The vehicle is preparing for takeoff."

"Take that stuff, Ernie. I'll get the rest," she said. "And tell Joe if he doesn't stop yelling over that thing, I'm going to take his head off!"

"I'll be sure to tell him, Sheriff."

Sharyn muttered to herself as she threw her things together. She was glad that she'd slept in her long cotton sweatpants and T-shirt. She'd taken a swim in shorts early that morning in a small lake. She was grateful they hadn't come up then.

With her arms full, she ran under the helicopter blades and threw her stuff into the interior. Ernie grabbed it and stashed it with the rest in the cargo area.

"This had better be important," she stressed again when she had pushed herself into the helicopter behind her possessions. "I can't believe you brought the helicopter up here."

"It seemed like the best way to find you fast, Sheriff," Joe told her with a grin. "That's what it's for, isn't it?"

"For finding lost hikers and children," she agreed. "I don't think I fit either group."

"You *are* the Sheriff!" Joe huffed.

"With Ty Swindoll on our backs about spending money?" she questioned. "If he gets wind of this, he's going to blow it up big. So, this had better be important."

She glanced from one deputy's face to the other as the helicopter took off from the mountain.

"Tom Metzger is missing," Ernie told her.

"Tom . . . oh, the man looking for the plane in the lake?" she recalled.

Ernie nodded. "He's been gone for the past two days."

"Maybe he's just trying to take a vacation for a few days," she retorted, then sighed. "You've looked for him?"

"Everywhere."

"We've done tactical and aerial searches for him," Joe explained.

Sharyn shook her head. When Joe came back from his two weeks with the National Guard every year, it was like he'd stepped out of a commando movie.

"Any sign of foul play?" she wondered, scratching at a spot on her leg where something had bitten her.

"None that we can find," Ernie replied. "His truck is missing and the guys with the crane are here, setting up to try to get the plane out of the lake. They said he was supposed to be here."

"And his brother's here," Joe told her.

"His brother?"

"John Metzger. Colonel. Retired from the Green Berets, the FBI, and the CIA, along with a year with the Secret Service protecting the President of the United States at the White House," Joe completed, obviously impressed.

Sharyn looked at them. "You're having trouble with the man's brother, aren't you?"

Ernie scratched his wisp of hair. "He's a little hostile."

"He's threatening to bring in the FBI," Joe explained.

"He can threaten," Sharyn answered. "But without some sign of kidnaping or force being used against him, they probably wouldn't come in on the case. He needs to be missing for more than just a few days."

"Tom Metzger is a pretty famous author," Ernie reminded her. "He won the Pulitzer for that story he did on the Marines in Vietnam a few years back."

"And Colonel Metzger obviously has ties to the Bureau," Joe reminded her.

Sharyn shrugged. "Well, I'm off the mountain now. I guess it won't hurt to take a look at it."

"Sorry, Sheriff," Ernie apologized again. "I didn't know what else to do. I know it was your first vacation in two years. We just couldn't cope with this man. He keeps demanding to see the sheriff."

"It's okay," she assured him. "We'll sort it out and if there's time, I'll go back until the end of the week."

They landed the helicopter on the roof of the court-house. The EMS tech pilot waved. He smiled at the sight of Sharyn's black sweatpants with large red hearts on them.

The helicopter was new, bought only a few months before when the state passed a law that all large counties with mountains and lakes had to own a helicopter. Their machine had to be shared between emergency, law enforcement, and medical teams. They were working on a member of the Sheriff's office learning to fly the beast but to begin with, there were only four Emergency Services techs certified to pilot it.

"What time is it, Ernie?" Sharyn wondered. She'd left her watch at home to forget about the demands of the job for the week.

"Almost eleven P.M.," Ernie obliged her. "I've got a car standing by to take you home so you can change clothes and meet with Colonel Metzger."

She nodded, not quite sure she understood how this had become a prominent missing persons case in such a short time. Tom Metzger was an adult. He could have gone anywhere without letting people know here he'd gone. Why all the fuss?

From what she could tell, it was more that his brother was worried about him and her deputies were intimidated by his brother. Joe pushed open the door that led to the back entrance through the impound lot and garage, and she immediately understood their problem.

Col. John Metzger was a formidable man. He was built like a tank with a hawk's beak of a nose and eyes the color and warmth of granite. His chin jutted out, square and clefted, like Superman's. He wore his full-dress uniform with enough medals on his broad chest to blind a driver in the sunlight. A black beret sat on the side of his head at a menacing slant.

"So, this is the sheriff," he acknowledged with a long, meaningful stare at her worn black T-shirt and black novelty sweatpants.

"This area is restricted," Joe told him, moving to put himself between the man and the sheriff.

"That's right," Ernie backed him up. "Off limits to anyone who isn't Sheriff's Department personnel."

"Don't play games with me!" the man bellowed. "You were trying to sneak your boss out of the building before I could meet her." He gave Sharyn another long look. "And seeing her, I can understand why."

Joe and Ernie stood protectively on either side of Sharyn. She stepped out from between them.

"I'm Sheriff Sharyn Howard," she introduced herself, putting out her hand to the other man.

He took it and squeezed tightly. Sharyn didn't flinch.

"It's about time."

"Even sheriffs take vacations, Captain Metzger," she informed him.

"*Colonel* Metzger," he told her pointedly. "My brother is missing and I want to know what you're going to do about it, Sheriff."

It wouldn't have been possible to invest any more

irritation or lack of respect in his tone. He bit out his words like he was taking off the end of a cheap cigar.

"Well, Colonel," she answered quietly, "I'm going to go home, take a hot shower, and change clothes. Then I'm going to review the case. If there is something more to do or something more that we find out, we will contact you. Leave your name and the number where you can be reached at the front desk."

"What?"

"My deputy will show you where that is, Colonel," she continued, unfazed by his shouting. "If you'll excuse me."

Joe nodded, standing his ground, while Ernie walked with Sharyn to the end of the corridor that led to the parking lot.

"It figures a woman wouldn't have the stomach for working a job like this," the colonel sneered.

Sharyn turned back to him. "My deputy will be glad to escort you back to the front of the building, sir. And if you haven't given a statement, he'll be glad to take it."

"I've given a statement!"

"Then I suggest you wait to hear from us on this matter, sir. We'll be in touch. Good night."

The colonel was beyond words. He turned on his heel and plowed through the door that led back into the front office like an enraged bull. Joe followed him.

"Wow!" Ernie said, opening the door for her. "That was something!"

"Something?" she demanded. "Is that what you brought me back for?"

Ernie shook his head. "You know me better. I wouldn't have brought you back just to deal with that bully. I don't like the way this whole thing is going, Sheriff. I felt like you needed to be here."

Sharyn climbed into the patrol car. "You think something's happened to Mr. Metzger?"

"Maybe."

She sighed and leaned her head back against the seat while Ernie drove them through the dark streets of Diamond Springs. The mostly clapboard houses that surrounded the lake and lined the streets huddled together like old ladies at a funeral. The town had seen its ups and downs. Mill closings that crippled the town for years. Boom times that had built some of the stately mansions that graced the hills.

"Get everyone together who's done anything on the case so far," she told him. "We'll meet in an hour at the office."

"David's with his fiancée tonight and Trudy's with her grandbaby," Ernie explained.

"And I'm on vacation," Sharyn told him bluntly. "Tell Trudy she can bring her grandbaby and David can bring his fiancée. This shouldn't take long."

Sharyn was surprised to see that the lights were still on in the driveway at her house. She knew her mother wasn't expecting her back until the end of the week and her sister, Kristie, was spending the summer building Habitat for Humanity homes in Arkansas. Her mother had a thing about leaving the lights on and wasting electricity.

Ernie walked in with her. The door was locked and there was no sign of her mother. At that time of night, her absence was even stranger than her leaving on the lights. If she wasn't back by the time they were ready to go, Sharyn decided that she would make a few phone calls.

"I wonder where my mother is?" she said aloud. "She's never out after dark."

"I haven't seen her this week," Ernie told her. "I can call around."

"No, that's okay," Sharyn replied. "Let's get going on this Metzger thing and I'll worry about my mother later."

Ernie made coffee and started calling in the troops while Sharyn went to her bedroom to shower and change.

It had been embarrassing to be caught in those tacky sweatpants by a man who owed respect and allegiance to uniforms. It would have been nice to get out of the building without meeting him, but what was done was done. It was too late for regrets.

All she could do was remember what her father had taught her about men who bullied those around them. Look them in the eye. Never show fear or weakness. Treat them with respect but make sure they respect the law.

Sharyn had done the best she could in the situation but it had been a bad first meeting. It would give him the upper hand at subsequent meetings. When he looked at her, he would see her in those sweatpants. It was unfortunate but not something that she was going to let bother her. The man had obviously enjoyed bullying her deputies while she was gone. She wasn't going to give him the satisfaction of bullying her.

The hot shower removed any last vestiges of her vacation. She'd been in the mountains for two glorious days. She knew she'd been lucky to get those. She dried her copper-colored curls, looking at the slight sunburn she'd managed to acquire on her face and neck. It made her look a little less pasty-faced and complimented her longer hairstyle.

She'd been experimenting with letting her hair grow out a little longer. She'd kept it short since her father had died. Not that the two events were related, beyond her taking his job when they'd held the special election after his death. She hadn't really expected to become sheriff. There had never been a woman sheriff in Diamond Springs, North Carolina.

A lot of people said that she had won the election because everyone felt sorry for her after her father was murdered during a local convenience-store robbery. Sharyn tried to look at it as an opportunity to show them that she could do as good a job as her father and her grandfather before him. If she'd been his son, they would've felt it was passed down through the family.

She dried herself and started to dress. Her uniform had just returned from the dry cleaners. She pulled it from its plastic wrapper.

The brown-and-tan uniform was cut along square lines to fit a man's body. Sharyn pulled on the pants and shirt. Her body was always fighting a losing battle to stay within the sheriff's guidelines for weight. The uniform couldn't have looked worse on her.

As she picked up her grandfather's service revolver that she carried in a holster at her side, there was a knock at the door.

"When did you get home?" her mother asked sweetly, coming in and closing the door.

"About half an hour ago," Sharyn replied. "I was surprised you were out so late."

Faye Howard blushed prettily. She was still a very attractive woman. The charm and beauty that won her several beauty queen crowns in her youth were still apparent in her face and voice.

"I didn't expect you back so soon."

"Where were you?" Sharyn asked, trying to button the cuffs on her shirt.

Her mother pushed her hand away and buttoned the right cuff. "I was out on a date."

"A date?" Sharyn asked, surprised. She didn't know her mother dated.

"Yes," her mother confirmed, buttoning the left cuff. "With Caison Talbot."

"Caison?"

Faye looked at her daughter's astonished face. "Yes. Caison. We've been friends for so long. His own dear Marcy has been dead for ten years. Why would our dating be such a surprise?"

"Mother, Caison Talbot is . . ."

"Yes?" Her mother waited.

Sharyn couldn't find the words without being incredibly rude. "You know what I mean."

"I know that you and Caison have not always seen eye-to-eye, Sharyn," her mother acknowledged. "But he and I get along quite well."

"How long have you been dating him?" Sharyn wondered, putting her gun in her holster.

"About three months," her mother replied, eyeing her daughter's slightly overweight body in the police uniform with a critical eye. "You know, Sharyn, if you lost just ten pounds, that uniform would look so much better on you."

Sharyn grimaced. "Thanks. Is this thing with you and Caison serious?"

Faye shrugged her delicate shoulders. "Who can

tell, dear? We'll just have to see. Ernie told me about this crisis of yours."

Sharyn wanted to ask, *Which one?* The idea that there could be something between her mother and Senator Caison Talbot was crisis enough for her!

"I don't think it's necessarily something serious," she told her mother. "I think Tom Metzger's brother is a bully and my deputies didn't know what to do."

"You know, Sharyn," her mother told her, "I've never approved of you doing this job. It's a job for a man. Not a pretty, intelligent woman."

"I know, Mother."

"You should be thinking about getting married and having babies. You're not getting any younger."

"I know, Mother." How many times had they had this discussion?

"Men are going to find it hard to get close to you in that uniform, carrying a gun and doing all the distasteful things you have to do."

"You married Dad," she reminded her mother.

Faye sighed for her wayward daughter. "That was different, Sharyn. A woman needs a man she can look up to. A man she can respect and feel safe with. Men aren't looking for that. They want a woman who will cook and take care of them. Not a sheriff who arrests drunks and almost gets strangled!"

Sharyn put on her hat, looking in the mirror to find the best possible location for its flat brim on top of her springy red curls.

"If I do get married, Mother, he'll have to find this uniform attractive and he won't care that I don't cook."

"Dressed like that, Sharyn Howard," her mother informed her brutally, "you will never find a husband!"

Sharyn smiled and opened the door. "Maybe not. But maybe I can find Tom Metzger."

Ernie handed her a travel mug of coffee as she walked into the kitchen.

"Everybody's on their way," he reported, nodding to Faye then looking at Sharyn.

"Good. Let's get going."

Sharyn's mother shook her head. "Ernie, you've known Sharyn since she was a baby. Talk to her. Tell her she's not going to get married if she keeps this job."

Ernie glanced between the two women. "Uh . . . yes, ma'am."

"Thank you. You've always been a good friend."

"Thank you, ma'am," he replied, avoiding Sharyn's eyes.

"See you later, Mother," Sharyn said, leaving the house.

"Good night, Sharyn."

"Trouble?" Ernie asked as they walked out to the car.

"My mother is dating Caison Talbot and she wants me to get married and have babies and give up being sheriff. Besides that, no."

"Senator Talbot?" Ernie whistled between this teeth. "Imagine having him for a stepdaddy!"

Sharyn shuddered. "No, thanks."

"It could happen," Ernie teased her. "I could see that look in your mama's eyes."

"What look?" she demanded, getting into the car beside him.

He waggled his eyebrows on his thin face. "You know what look. She's already picking out her china patterns."

"Never mind that," she answered shortly, not wanting to think about it. "Tell me about Tom Metzger."

Ernie started the car and obliged her.

"He went missing two days ago. His brother came to the office and told us that he was supposed to meet him at his hotel Sunday but he hadn't seen anything of him. There was no note. His rental truck is gone. The divers and crane operator who are supposed to bring the plane up out of the lake came yesterday and waited all day for him. He was supposed to meet them at the site."

"Have you called around?"

He nodded. "I called the rental company where he got the truck. He hadn't turned it back in. I filed a report with the DMV to look for the vehicle but so far there haven't been any reports of him or the truck."

"But no sign of foul play?" she finished.

"None at all. We looked over the site. It looked like he finished up for the day and went home. No sign of a struggle at his motel room. Everything seems just as it should. Except that he's gone."

She glanced at him in the passing streetlight's glare. "But you have a feeling about it?"

He nodded. "Yes, I do."

"You think something happened to him?"

"I don't know, Sheriff. He's gone. No one knows where. I don't like it."

"All right. That's good enough for me."

"So, you're not mad that I brought you back from your vacation?"

Sharyn frowned. "I didn't say that. But I'm not mad at you, Ernie. Just mad."

"I can understand those sentiments, Sheriff. Indeed, I can."

The three deputies who made up the Diamond Springs sheriff's office were waiting when they got there. Trudy, the office director, was there with her grandson, a lively two-year-old named Mark. She had already pulled out her files on the case and found a place for David's fiancée to wait until the meeting was over.

Joe was telling everyone about the sheriff's meeting with John Metzger that evening. They all looked up when she entered. The interrogation room that doubled as their meeting room grew suspiciously quiet.

"Sorry to bring you boys in," Sharyn apologized at the beginning.

"I can't believe we're investigating this thing," David was quick to point out. "The man's missing but it hasn't been proven that he was taken forcibly or injured by anyone."

Sharyn took her place at the scarred wooden table in the big room. "We don't know anything yet. Let's take a look at everything we have and decide where to go from here."

"I want to go home and go back to bed," Ed Robinson joked, his blue eyes laughing.

"What for?" Joe asked with a short laugh. "No amount of beauty sleep's gonna help you!"

"I'm prettier than you on a good day," Ed replied, sweeping his hand back over his curly blond hair.

"Okay." Sharyn brought them back. "Have we canvassed the area? Made sure no one saw or heard anything unusual?"

"We talked to all the neighbors who live around the site on the lake. Two of them were on vacation. The others didn't see or hear anything. They remember seeing Metzger's red pickup there while he's been working at the site. They hadn't even noticed that it was gone for the past few days," Ed told her with a yawn.

"And the hotel clerk?"

"Metzger was paid up through the end of the month. He came and went all the time," Joe explained. "He didn't think anything of it and he didn't notice anything different."

"What about his publisher or his agent? If he had travel plans, surely they'd know?"

Ernie shook his head. "Couldn't get in touch with the agent. He's out of the country. But the publisher didn't know of any travel plans. He told me that Metzger has a habit of wandering off for a while sometimes."

"Great," David expressed.

Sharyn glanced at him. "What about family? Is this brother it?"

David shrugged. "As far as any of us could find." He consulted his notebook. "He gives his place of residence as New York City. He has an apartment there but no one's seen him for a while. His landlord says he has a tendency to wander as well."

Sharyn nodded and considered the possibilities.

"Let's put out an all-points bulletin for him and the truck. Ernie, find out where the agent is staying out of the country and keep trying until you get him. He's probably the most likely to know if Metzger's traveling on business."

"Yes, ma'am."

"David, let's see if we can find out if he has any friends he could be visiting."

He groaned and closed his notebook.

"Tomorrow is soon enough," she added, knowing

she was about to hear a protest. "Joe, Ed, take the neighbors around the lake again and find out if they noticed anything strange before he disappeared."

"Tomorrow?" Joe asked hopefully.

Sharyn nodded. "So far as we can tell, nothing has happened to this man. People who know him say he has a tendency to wander. His brother probably just overreacted. I don't see any reason to make this urgent yet. If he's in any danger, we can't find it."

"What about the colonel?" Ernie wondered.

"I'll tackle him tonight," she told him. "If people are used to his brother wandering away, how could he be so sure he'd be here when he got here to see him? He might just be irritated that he wasn't here. Trudy, if you could get me his address?"

"Sure thing, Sheriff."

"Then I guess you can all go home. Or wherever. I want to hear when you finish your reports on this tomorrow. See you then."

"Want some moral support?" Ernie asked her as the others were leaving the room.

"Thanks," she answered with a smile. "But I'd better do this alone. If you come with me, he's just going to see me as not being able to cope with him alone. See you tomorrow."

Ernie frowned. "Sheriff—"

"I'll be fine, Ernie. Go home!"

He sighed. "Yes, ma'am."

"She's not a bit afraid of him, is she?" Ed asked as they watched her walk out of the building.

"That's why she's the sheriff," Ernie told them quietly.

"But you wish she'd let you go, right?" Joe asked, slapping Ernie on the back.

Ernie glanced up at him, then looked away. "Good night. See ya'll tomorrow."

Chapter Two

It was almost midnight when Sharyn reached the motel where Col. John Metzger was staying. It was the big one they'd built where the new highway was coming through, just outside town. Housing subdivisions clustered along the route that ran like ribbon back to Charlotte. Fast-food chains and gas stations, advertising everything from coffee to movie rentals, were going up faster than the road itself.

The road and the ensuing commercial climate had changed many people's lives. Farms that had been worked by the same families for five generations were lost to the need to live outside the city, yet still be able to commute. Oaks over two hundred years old had fallen beneath the grinding onslaught of prosperity.

The county was changing. Everyone had to face it. Ty Swindoll had come from one of the new communities to take the place of George Albert when he retired his commission seat and left the area after his son's death. The rural districts of the county had never involved themselves in politics or worried about much of anything except the price of feed and fencing. Suddenly the newcomers from the city were everywhere, demanding that things change to accommodate them and their upscale lives.

Ty Swindoll had won the special election for George Albert's seat on the platform of change and reform. He questioned every penny that was spent by the county and demanded that more be spent on the "necessities" that the new communities were facing. That included new parks, more paved roads, and after-school programs for children.

Sharyn had ignored it, for the most part. She figured it would pass. Until he'd started calling for belt tightening in the sheriff's department.

She parked the patrol car in the space in front of number 226 at the motel. She wasn't looking forward to seeing the colonel so soon after their last clash. And it wasn't that she wasn't used to taking personal jibes about being a woman in a man's job. He was just the kind of man who went out of his way to promote the fact that he liked to push people around. He would always be stronger and smarter.

In short, she thought as she straightened her shoulders and knocked on the door, *The man is obnoxious.*

"Well," the colonel said as he opened the door to his motel room. "Look who it is! The good sheriff of Diamond Springs. This time with her pretty badge shining and a big bad gun."

"May I come in?" she asked, removing her hat and holding on to her temper in fractions.

"Of course. Come in. Make yourself comfortable."

She looked around the room. The colors were sub-
dued, mauve and pale green. Everything had a smell
of newness to it. The smell of new carpets and new
furniture and air-conditioning. The bed was made up
neatly and there was no sign of any of the colonel's
belongings.

"Did you find him?" he asked immediately. His bru-
tal eyes were on her freckled face and curly red hair.

"Not yet, sir," she replied firmly, not looking away
from him. "But I feel sure we will. In the meantime,
I'd like to ask you a few questions."

"Shoot!" he answered, standing against the wall
with his arms folded across his broad chest. "Pick my
brain, Sheriff."

Sharyn had to admit that he looked far less intimi-
dating without his full uniform. The gold braid and the
mountain of medals were guaranteed to quell even the
most courageous heart. In his shirtsleeves and khakis
he looked a lot like anybody else. Except that his face
was carved from rock and his tone was cold enough
to cut to the bone.

Sharyn laid her hat on the bed and took out her
notebook and pencil.

"When were you supposed to meet your brother?"

"Three days ago. He wanted me to be here when
he brought up the plane. I'm an expert on World War
Two devices. I was going to help him with the new
book he was writing on the whole thing."

"You're a writer too, then?" she asked scribbling in
her pad.

"No. Just a military man who knows his way around
guns and machinery. His book that won the Pulitzer
was an account of my time in Vietnam. Most people
don't know that."

"Your, uh, brother wasn't in Vietnam then?"

"My brother was a coward. He still is. He'd rather write about war then experience it. He didn't run to Canada but he found ways to stay here while everyone else was doing the dangerous stuff. Then he wrote about it."

"So, you weren't close?"

"We had a difference of opinion," he told her. "Don't you disagree occasionally with your family?"

She nodded. "I'm sure everyone does. Can you think of any place your brother might have gone? A regular getaway place? Maybe somewhere he went to be alone?"

The colonel snorted and moved away from the wall. "I wouldn't be here talking to you at midnight if I could think of where he was myself, Sheriff. That's *your* job."

Sharyn ignored the barbed remark and continued, wanting to get it over.

"His publisher and his landlord in New York both claim that he's the kind of man who likes to wander away. Do you think that's a fair assessment?"

"I suppose so," John Metzger admitted. "He's never wandered away when he was supposed to meet me, but there has been a change in his life recently."

"Oh?" she questioned, glancing up at him. "What's that, Colonel?"

"A woman, of course. Not being a man, I doubt you'd understand what a change that can make in a man's life, Sheriff. You'll have to take it from me that it can be profound."

"So, he's been seeing a new woman?"

"Exactly." He nodded curtly. "But don't ask me her name. We were never introduced."

"Why would that be, sir?" she asked.

The colonel smiled a deadly, predatory smile. "Because every woman Tom ever had, I took away from him at some point. He got to where he didn't introduce me anymore, if he wanted to keep the woman."

"I see," she remarked, continuing to scribble.

"Do you, Sheriff?" he questioned. "Are you capable of discerning the drab from the dross?"

She looked up at him. "I'd like to think so."

He studied her face then nodded, as though satisfied with what he saw there. "I see you carry an older weapon, Sheriff Howard. I think I recognize it. Mind if I take a look?"

Sharyn glanced at the service revolver at her side then took it out and handed it carefully to him. "It was my grandfather's weapon during World War Two."

He weighed the gun with his hand. "It's a good weapon, Sheriff. Shoots straight and true. The kind of weapon a man can rest his life on."

He handed it back to her and Sharyn breathed again. She put away her notes and thanked him.

"I hope we'll have something for you tomorrow, Colonel. And if you think of anything else, please let us know."

"I certainly will, Sheriff," he said, offering her his hand.

She took it warily but this time he was careful, squeezing her hand lightly then looking at her fingers and palm.

"You know, Sheriff," he said, not looking up at her, "You and I are a lot a like. Those men of yours, I couldn't respect them. What you did, coming here tonight, took guts. That must be why you're in charge."

"I just won the election," she replied, taking her

hand from him. She put her hat on her head, then turned back to him. "Oh, one more thing."

"Yes, Sheriff?"

"When did you say you noticed your brother was missing?"

"When I arrived, expecting to meet him."

"And that was?"

He smiled but the result wasn't friendly. "Am I a suspect in my brother's disappearance? After everything I've done just to get you people to investigate?"

"They pay me to ask the questions," she told him. "Nothing personal, Colonel Metzger."

"I got here Monday morning," he replied coldly. "We were supposed to meet about six A.M. I drove straight down from D.C. I have receipts from the places I stopped along the way. Good enough?"

"Thanks." She nodded. "You can give those to my deputy at the office. I'll let you know if we find out anything new."

"You do that, Sheriff. Sharyn, wasn't it? Maybe we can have a drink together, Sharyn."

"I appreciate the offer," she told him. "But I'm sure you'd rather me spend my time finding your brother."

"Spoken like a true leader!" he complimented her. "I know your father was proud of you."

The man was a shark, caged in by rules and regulations, but it didn't make his teeth any less sharp. Sharyn nodded to him casually and left him there. But she felt his eyes on her back as she walked away.

"The way he expressed it," she told Ernie the next morning, "he enjoyed taking his brother's girlfriends away."

"Power," Ernie told her, sipping his coffee. "That kind of man. It's all about power."

Ernie had finally connected with Tom Metzger's agent sometime early that morning. The agent had underscored the fact that while Tom was devoted to his projects, he also had to have frequent breaks. Sometimes he'd be gone for weeks and suddenly show up again. While it might be a little unusual that he disappeared in the middle of a project, there could have been extenuating circumstances.

"Like a woman?" Sharyn wondered aloud in the middle of the busy coffee shop.

Ernie shrugged. "He wouldn't go into it any further. Just to say that it didn't surprise him that Mr. Metzger was missing."

"The colonel told me last night that there was a new woman in his brother's life. He claimed not to know her because his brother was afraid he would have taken her away."

Ernie shrugged his thin shoulders. "It all sounds like I brought you down from the mountain for nothing, Sheriff."

"That's okay," she told him with a smile. "You were doing your job."

"Is this private or can anyone join in on slamming the sheriff?"

Sharyn looked up. "I didn't know you ever needed an invitation to give me a hard time, Nick," she said as he took a seat across from her, beside Ernie.

He pulled out the *Diamond Springs Gazette* and laid it out on the table for her. On the front page was the full story about the missing author/archaeologist and his brother's account of what little the sheriff's department was doing to find him.

"I thought you were on vacation." Nick asked.

"I was." She grimaced. "Until this came up."

"If you love page one," he assured her with a grin, "you're gonna love page two."

Sharyn opened the paper and there was an editorial by Ty Swindoll that featured pictures of Sharyn in her heart-covered sweatpants leaving the helicopter on the courthouse roof.

" 'The sheriff travels in style. Expensive style,' " she read aloud.

Ernie glanced at the paper, then shook his head. "Some people don't have anything better to do than look for trouble."

Sharyn closed the paper and looked at Nick. "I suppose this made your heart sing."

"Me?" he asked. "I don't like it when other people give you a hard time, Sharyn. I like to reserve that special place for myself."

"Talk about people with no lives," she returned. "I suppose there's nothing as lonely as a medical examiner with no dead bodies to examine."

"I make up for it with cadavers at the college," he replied quickly. "You should come over one night. I could show you the ropes."

"That's your job," she assured him. "I don't need it."

"Seriously." Nick returned to the subject of her vacation. "You came back for a missing person?"

She shrugged and Ernie cringed.

"It might be more than that."

"Really?" Nick rested his chin on his hand and looked at her sunburned face. "Tell me more."

"There isn't anything definite yet," she answered, a little flustered by his intense scrutiny of her face.

"Yet, here you are, giving up your vacation," he said thoughtfully. "Or maybe it has something to do with a picture I saw on page ten."

"What else?" she asked as Ernie opened the newspaper.

"Aw, Sheriff." Ernie tsked, shaking his head and handing her the paper.

It was the society page. There was a picture of her mother dancing with Caison Talbot at a local charity event.

"Are you about to have a new daddy?" Nick asked with a smile.

Ernie sipped his coffee. "You're gonna have to do something about the quality of the men in your life, Sheriff."

Nick glanced at him, then at Sharyn, who was making faces at her deputy.

"What did I miss?"

Sharyn told him briefly about the colonel and his predatory handshakes. "You shouldn't have gone there alone," Nick, suddenly serious, expressed at once.

"That's what I told her," Ernie agreed.

"I'm the sheriff," she argued. "I can't back down from every man who acts like he wants to devour me for dinner that night."

"No," Nick argued, his dark eyes intent. "But you could shoot them."

Ernie laughed out loud.

"She *is* the sheriff," Nick suggested.

"I could shoot you too," she retorted with a laugh.

Ed Robinson came around the line at the front counter and stood at the side of their table. His curly blond hair was mussed and his blue eyes were shadowed.

"You need to come down to the lake, Sheriff. I think we might have found Tom Metzger."

"Alive?" she asked hopefully.

Ed shrugged and looked away. "Probably not."

"Great," she muttered, standing. She tossed away her coffee cup. "I guess we found something for you to do too, Nick. No more lonely nights."

Somehow, she was bringing up the rear, walking beside Nick, with Ernie and Ed in the front, as they went out of the coffee shop.

As they walked out the door, Nick put his on her arm to hold her back. She looked at him. They were almost on the same eye level.

"Be careful, Sharyn. I met this guy. He's a loose cannon."

"I'm always careful," she replied, her voice a little breathless. "But thanks."

Nick moved his hand. "I'll get my car and notify the hospital staff, then I'll meet you down there."

"All right," she answered, watching him leave. Ernie called her name twice to get her attention.

"What have you got, Ed?" she asked at once, getting into the patrol car.

"Nan Bellows was out fishing early this morning. She pulled up some shirt material and a hat, then we found some stuff washed up on the shore."

"What kind of stuff?" Ernie asked, taking the car carefully through the crowded streets.

Ed shrugged. "Some kind of machinery. The guys are out there with the crane, ready to pull up the plane. They said it looked like some underwater gizmos that Mr. Metzger might have used to help locate the plane."

"Couldn't he have just left them there?" Sharyn wondered.

"They're full of water, Sheriff. Looks like they've been under for a while."

"Not that it proves Metzger is under there," Ernie argued for the sake of it.

They reached the site off the gravel road that ran along the lake. Sharyn unfastened her seat belt and took a deep breath.

Ty Swindoll was going to love this!

The heavy crane was set up right next to the lake. Two men were suited up in dark-colored scuba gear, waiting in a boat offshore. A crowd had gathered because the paper had advertised the day and time the plane was going to be brought up out of the murky depths of the lake. Unfortunately, it had worked out to be the same time Nan had made her discovery.

Sharyn considered clearing the beach but she felt it would draw even more unwanted attention to the situation. Instead, she decided to play down the sheriff's department's role. Let the crowd think they were there to assist the salvage operation.

Ed had radioed ahead for Joe to meet them there. Together, they put up yellow police tape to form a barrier that the growing crowd would stand behind. With the addition of the sheriff and soon after, the medical examiner and ambulance, the crowd grew like the mist coming off of the lake.

Diamond Mountain Lake was a popular resort area on the weekends. Fishermen and swimmers, and lately children on power skis, took advantage of the long, wide shoreline. The lake was created and fed by the merging of two rivers. Further up from Diamond Springs, the power company had built a dam that helped control flooding and produced hydroelectric power.

There had been talk for years about putting a nuclear power plant there but so far it had just been talk. On the lakes around Charlotte where there were nuclear facilities, there was talk of three-headed fish and frogs with six legs. No one in the area wanted that for their lake.

Sharyn waited for the divers to come in from the boat. Ed had already bagged the scrap of shirt Nan had pulled up from the lake. There was still a hook and a piece of nylon fishing cord embedded in it. The baseball cap was as nondescript as the material. It could have belonged to anyone.

Nick took the cap in the plastic bag from her. "I think that might be blood on the cap."

"Where?" Sharyn asked, looking at it again.

The cap was red and it was difficult to see but there was a stain of some sort on the white sweatband on the inside.

"Here." She handed him the piece of material and the fish hook. "You might as well have this too."

The divers nodded to them. "It's pretty hard to see the bottom of the lake. It's no wonder they couldn't find the plane all those years ago. There's a lot of debris and silt."

"Did you see anything else?" Sharyn asked.

They glanced at each other. "We put the hooks on the plane, then we came up. But we could go back down and take another look."

"That would be great, thanks," Sharyn replied. "You can send my deputy your invoice for the job. He'll give you the address."

"Will do, Sheriff."

"Where are we looking?" the other diver asked.

Sharyn glanced around but didn't see Nan Bellows. "Hold on a minute."

She walked back toward the crowd. Some people shouted at her. She recognized a few of them and waved back. The single newspaper writer from the *Gazette* was there. He took her picture. Sharyn glanced at him and wondered if he'd taken her picture when she was getting off the helicopter. Somehow, she didn't think Ty Swindoll did his own work. Just instigated others.

Nan Bellows was having a cup of coffee with Ed as he took her statement. Sharyn shook hands with her. Nan smiled and offered her a doughnut.

"Brought these with me for breakfast. Fish like 'em too."

"Thanks." Sharyn accepted a greasy doughnut. "So, what happened this morning, Nan?"

"I came out about four, like I always do. Best fishin' then, you know. Cool, too. Fish don't like it when it gets hot like this."

"So, you were out in your boat, fishing?"

"Yeah. I put my pole in a few times and caught one or two little ones. I was after a few big ones for the Davises for supper. Pay real good."

She took a bite of doughnut and then smiled at the sheriff.

"I put the pole in again, a little deeper, then it got caught on somethin'. I heaved and heaved. It finally come up. It was that hat I gave your man over there."

"Then you pulled up the material?"

"That's right, Sheriff. The line caught again and this time it snapped, but when I looked back, there it was, floatin' on the water just like a cloud!"

A television camera crew van from the local station went slowly by them. Gravel spit out from under the tires and dust flew up into the moist air.

"Where were you, Nan?" Sharyn asked, ignoring them.

"I was about where I always am, Sheriff. Just off the boat ramp over there. Fish like it 'cause of the weeds on the sides."

"Thanks, Nan," Sharyn said, taking a five-dollar bill out of her pocket. "Here's for the hook. I appreciate you saving it for us."

Nan grinned toothlessly. " 'Welcome, Sheriff. You're a good 'un. Always said so."

Sharyn thanked her and walked back to where Nick, Ernie, and the divers were talking.

"Nan says she was fishing off the boat ramp there." She pointed. "If you could take a look around that area."

The divers nodded and went back to their boat. The buzz of the people waiting to see something happen was beginning to rival the cicadas singing in the trees around the lake. The sun was hot already and it was barely 10:00 in the morning. It would be oppressive by afternoon.

"I told them not to touch whatever they found down there," Nick said to her. He ran his hand through his gray-laced, jet-black hair. "If he's down there, I'll have to go down."

"That's right." She turned to him thoughtfully. "The medical examiner has to be on the scene before the body can be moved."

"And there might be something down there with him that could make the case."

Ernie glanced at Nick. "You don't look so good, compadre. You get a little queasy in the water?"

Nick shook his head. "I'm not much of a water person, I guess."

Sharyn couldn't believe that Nick was afraid of the water! He had always been remote, fearless, and critical of everything she did. She wasn't used to thinking of him any other way.

Thinking about his hand on her arm and his warning about the colonel made him seem almost human. Seeing the fear in his eyes as he looked at the lake's placid surface made him vulnerable for once.

"Maybe we'll all catch a break and there won't be anything down there." Sharyn filled in the taut silence while they waited. "I don't need another murder investigation so soon."

Ernie folded his arms across his chest and looked out at the water. It was beginning to fill up with boaters, flashing across the waves in the sun. Diamond Mountain was a brooding giant across the lake, rising against the blue sky.

"It could be anything with all the people out here every day this summer."

Ed joined them near the top of the boat ramp. "Anything yet?"

"They've only been down a few minutes," Sharyn apprised him.

"I took Nan's statement and sent her home," he told her.

"There was no reason for her to stay," Sharyn agreed, her eyes fixed on the small green boat bobbing up and down at the end of the boat ramp.

The crane started up and all eyes swiveled toward

it. The operator saluted the crowd and the television camera, then he turned to the prize under the lake.

The heavy cables strained at the hooks that had been placed on the old plane, invisible under the water. The operator changed gears and positions of the rig but the cables still strained and smoked.

Sharyn thought about the old legend. Everyone knew it but most thought it was *just* a legend. Until Tom Metzger came to town.

It was a love story, of sorts. Tragic. Something to sigh over on a long summer's evening.

Captain Billy Bost had been flying back to the war at the beginning of 1944. He'd been gone for a long time and he wasn't permitted to stop off and see his lady love before being reassigned.

The town was called Palmer then. Named for Palmer Mountain and Palmer Lake. Old Man Palmer had been a wealthy, eccentric businessman looking for a place to hide away after his wife's death. He built the first house on the lake. Probably put the first pontoon on the water.

It was still Palmer when Billy Bost told his love that he couldn't stop to see her. He grew up in Palmer. The war took its toll on the small town. Over a hundred young men were lost on foreign shores. Billy didn't know if he would ever come home. He wanted to let his fiancée know that he loved her and missed her.

He told her to watch the sky on that day in March. He was going to make a small detour, fly low, and dip his wings to signal to her that he was thinking about her and would return when he could. The story said that the plane flew too low and he lost control of it. The plane plunged into the lake and was never seen again. The bodies of Captain Billy Bost and his copilot were never found.

The captain's lady, whose name was lost like her beloved and his plane, threw herself into the lake and drowned. Her body was never recovered, either.

Sharyn couldn't recall how Tom Metzger had found out about the local legend or what made him believe that it was true. She'd spoken to him briefly when he'd first come to town and requested a permit to excavate the lake. He was a personable man. A little tense. A little too used to getting his own way, with his Pulitzer Prize.

He'd given her a book that she had tried to read and had to give up. Too much murder and mayhem. She was a closet romance reader. Happy endings and pretty faces.

The divers were climbing back aboard the green boat. It rocked under their weight and movement in the choppy water.

"Here we go," Ernie said quietly. He wiped his forehead with a checkered handkerchief.

Sharyn glanced at Nick. There were small beads of perspiration forming on his upper lip. She looked away. The last thing she needed to do was feel sorry for Nick Thomopolis!

The boat dropped the divers off at the edge of the ramp that led into the water. They plodded up to their waiting reception party. Behind them, the crowd continued to watch the crane as it pulled and strained to bring up the plane.

"It's bad, Sheriff," the first diver to reach her proclaimed. He wiped his wet face with an equally wet hand. "There's a truck down there."

"With a man inside," the other diver added solemnly.

"We didn't touch anything, just like you said," the first diver told Nick.

Sharyn shook her head. "What color was the truck?"

"Red. Fire-engine red. The man is at the steering wheel, like he's driving. There's not much mud or debris. It must not have been down there for long."

Ernie took a deep breath and released it slowly.

Ed shook his head at Joe, who was still working the police line, keeping the growing crowd in check. Joe frowned and turned away.

"I'll have to go down," Nick said quickly. "Then we'll have to have it pulled out of there."

The divers nodded. "You can use one of our wet suits," one of them offered.

"Thanks," Nick replied tautly. "Thanks a lot."

"I'm going down with you," Sharyn said impulsively. She didn't want to spend too much time thinking about why she offered.

"That's crazy," Nick said, facing her. "Why would you?"

"I'm the sheriff," she told him quietly. "It's my job."

A huge cheer went up from the crowd behind them. As one, they turned to face the event. The crane was struggling but something was emerging from the water. Covered by fifty years of mud and plant life as well as debris from boaters and storms, the legendary plane of Captain Billy Bost was coming up into the sunlight again.

Chapter Three

Sharyn put on the wet suit in the MacKinzies' boat-house. The family had generously offered them the use of it for the investigation. The ramp was immediately down the hill from their house. They hadn't seen or heard anything but they had spoken with Tom Metzger on occasion when he'd been working at the site.

She was glad of two things. First, that she had gone scuba diving before in the lake, so she was familiar with what things looked like and how to use the gear. Second, that so far, the crowd was distracted by the plane being brought to the surface of the lake. They hadn't had time to wonder what else was going on.

Ed had already called a tow truck to pull the truck out of the water. After Nick's basic observation of the site, that would be the next step. It would be nice if the crowd had dispersed by that time, but the chances were that the shore would still be full of people.

She shook her head. Everyone was going to know

by tomorrow anyway. There was no way to keep a thing like that a secret. It was going to be a high-profile case since Metzger was a famous author and from out of town. It would be complicated because of that too. Trying to investigate a man's life who had no contacts in the community was going to be tough.

"I feel like a fish," Nick yelled through the paper-thin walls to her.

"I'm sure you look like a fish," she replied cheerfully.

"This stuff is hot," he complained.

She laughed. "It won't be underwater. Don't forget, the lake is spring-fed from the mountains as well as from the rivers. It stays pretty cool even in the summer."

"I wouldn't know."

"You've been here all these years and never went swimming?"

"Not once. I lived by the Atlantic Ocean in New Jersey but I never went swimming, either. If we were meant to swim in large bodies of water, we would have been born with gills."

Sharyn walked out into the sunshine and met him at the front of the boathouse.

"You do look like a fish," she told him briefly.

He nodded, his usually tan face looking a little gray. "Let's do this, huh?"

"Isn't there someone else?" she asked suddenly.

"Like who? A grad student from the college?"

"Who helps you with the autopsies? You don't work alone?"

"No one is qualified to do this, Sharyn. The state is pretty strict on being licensed. I'm sure Ty Swindoll wouldn't think there was enough crime around here to warrant an assistant for me."

She started to speak again, but he shook his head.

"I have to do this. Let's just get it over with."

"I'll be there," she said softly as she walked behind him toward the ramp where the green boat was waiting for them.

"What?"

She stopped. "I said, I'll be there. If you need help. I've dived before. I know the routine."

"Good for you." He snorted and walked away.

Not believing that she was fool enough to feel sorry for this man, she walked to the ramp and got into the boat. One of the other divers helped each of them with their masks and tanks, explaining how they worked and what they had to do.

The boat took them about a hundred yards off the ramp. The water was deep and full of weeds at that point. Perfect fishing, as Nan had pointed out.

Perfect to hide a truck, Sharyn guessed. The lake had been dredged at the edge of the ramp so that there was a steep drop-off, making it easier to launch a boat from that point. The truck would have gone down like a stone and the murky water would have hidden it forever.

Like Captain Bost's plane, she considered thoughtfully as she looked back at the plane. It was slowly moving toward the shore. Mud and slime dripped from it as it passed over the water.

"Ready?" the divers asked her and Nick.

Nick nodded. Sharyn looked at him, then nodded.

"Count to three," they said. "Then put in the mouthpiece and fall back into the water."

Sharyn remembered when her father had taken her

and her sister scuba diving at the end of the lake near the dam. The water was a little clearer there. He had picked that spot because the dam was interesting to view underwater.

Her mother and Caison Talbot had been there that day. Along with Talbot's wife, Marcy. The three of them had stayed on the boat and took in the hot sun and the white expanse of the dam while she and Kristie and her father had gone down.

Quickly, she put the memory out of her mind. She needed her wits about her in the water. And whether he liked it or not, Nick might need some help.

They fell back into the water together. Sharyn couldn't imagine how hard it must be for him to fall backward into the water, since he was afraid of it. The cold water closed around them and the bright sunlight was blotted out.

Sharyn clicked on her flashlight. The plants were thick around her and the light seemed to bounce off the long, waving fronds. She looked for Nick or his flashlight beam but didn't see anything. She swam to the left where he had gone over beside her.

She found him thrashing around in the water. He wasn't breathing and he didn't have his eyes open. His face was a mask of fear.

Immediately, she went to him and put her hands on either side of his head until he opened his eyes and looked at her. *"Breathe,"* she mimed. *"Through your mouth."* She pointed to her mouthpiece.

Nick nodded and stopped thrashing. He kicked his feet and took shallow breaths. He nodded that he was all right and she moved away from him. When she saw his flashlight beam, she knew it was okay.

The divers had left an underwater marker to find the

truck. When her flashlight beam picked it out, Sharyn swam toward it. She glanced back. Nick was right behind her.

The red truck came into view. It already looked as though it had been there for some time. It had a light coating of mud and debris. Even with the flashlight, Sharyn couldn't see in through the windshield. She swam around to the driver's side.

The window had been left down. Tom Metzger was sitting behind the wheel upright as though he had just driven down into the water and was waiting to drive back out. The water was holding his body upright though it was trapped by the seat belt across his chest and waist. A large swathe of his shirt was ripped away from the left arm where Nan must have hooked him.

Nick came up beside her. There were no marks on him. If that had been blood on his cap, there was no sign of it anywhere else. Of course, he had been under water for at least three days. Sharyn could only imagine that being in the water would hinder what they could learn from his body and the truck.

She waited beside him while Nick looked over everything in the truck and took some shots with a special camera. Then he shrugged and pointed to the surface. He had what he needed. He didn't want to be there longer than was necessary.

Sharyn watched as Nick fumbled with the camera and dropped the flashlight. The beam continued dropping until they couldn't see it in the dark plants anymore.

Between the plants and the cloudy water, Sharyn wasn't willing to take any chances. If she went up without him, he could panic again and they might not be able to find him. She had seen too many unfortunate accidents with good swimmers in the lake.

She motioned toward the surface, then took his hand and placed it on the belt around her waist. She curved his fingers around the belt, then nodded and started up.

Nick understood. He held on and went up with her. Face-to-face, they moved up into the sunlight.

They were only a few feet from the boat when they surfaced. Sun motes dappled the water and the warm air was welcome against their faces. The professional divers moved the boat closer to them and offered a hand getting over the side.

They took off the tanks and fins as the boat pushed close to the ramp. Sharyn was out of the boat and going up the ramp before Nick could follow. Ernie and Ed met her where the water stopped on the ramp.

"It was Metzger," she told them. "I'm going to change. Give Joe a hand with that crowd, Ed. We need it backed up farther. It's probably a long shot but maybe we can still find the tire track from his truck going to the ramp."

Ernie nodded. "Tow truck's here," he told her, following her to the door of the boathouse changing room.

"Hold off for now. Let's get what we can up here before we pull it up, Ernie."

"I'll get the crime kit that we got from the state."

She closed the door to the boathouse and stripped off the wet suit, drying herself quickly with the towel. She had a fine tremor to her hand and the start of an old-fashioned rage building in her chest as she stepped back into her uniform.

"Hey!" Nick called through the wall. "I suppose *that* was funny?"

"It wasn't funny at all," she told him bluntly. "It was stupid. If you had gone down there by yourself, you could have died."

"Just think of the years of insults you have to throw back in my face and what you can tell everyone about me being scared of water!"

"I'm too busy thinking about a dead man in the lake," she retorted pointedly as she tightened her holster and picked up her gun. "Get your report to me as soon as you can."

She slammed the door when she left the room, then dropped off the wet suit at the diver's boat. She didn't look back for Nick.

"Thanks," she said to the divers. "I appreciate your help."

"No problem," one of them told her. "Glad I don't have to see something like that every day."

"Who was he?" the other diver asked curiously.

"I can't say until his next of kin has been notified," she explained. "Sorry."

Tom Metzger's next of kin was at the lakeside. She saw him when she turned back toward the shore. He was working with another man and a woman, hosing down the plane that had been left on the shore. They were rubbing it carefully with large white rags as the water sluiced down the body and wings.

No time like the present, she considered, walking down the shore toward the plane.

The crane operator was packing up, loading his gear onto a large truck. The colonel was directing him around the side of the plane. The plane body was fragile. It had to be cleaned and preserved. One unintended slap of the crane's arm could demolish it.

"Colonel Metzger?" she called as she reached the plane.

He looked across the plane at her. "Sheriff." He nodded to the two people standing beside him. "This is Lieutenant Frank Wilkes and Captain Anne Parker."

"Sheriff," the lieutenant said as he and then the captain solemnly shook her hand. "We're part of the Navy's historical aviation corps. This is quite a find for us."

"I'm sure it is," Sharyn acknowledged briefly.

"My brother's lucky I waited around," the colonel told her. "If he had taken off and left the plane after it was brought up, it would have been ruined. Isn't it in great shape? I never imagined it would be so good."

"I need to speak with you, Colonel. I have information concerning your brother."

"Never mind. Just tell him to get back here and help me with this plane!"

Sharyn glanced at her shoes. "If you could come down, sir, I really need to speak with you in private."

The colonel looked at the two Naval officers who were busy working on the plane. "All right." He climbed down to where she stood at the edge of Diamond Mountain Lake's lapping water. "What is it that couldn't have waited, Sheriff?"

"We found your brother, Colonel Metzger." She studied his weathered face in the sunlight. "He's in the water."

"What?"

"He's in his truck, just off the ramp over there. Apparently the truck rolled into the water. I don't have all the details yet. But it looks as though he's been there for a few days."

"Dead? How is that possible, Sheriff?" he demanded. "Are you asking me to believe he fell asleep at the wheel and rolled off into the water? My brother is an excellent swimmer. He could have gotten out."

"As I said," she repeated, "I don't have all the details yet. We're going to be pulling out the truck in a short while. You're welcome to stay, if you like."

His mouth tightened and his eyes were hard as flint. "I'm sure I've seen worse, Sheriff."

"Is there anyone else in the family who should be contacted? We'd be willing to take care of it for you," she offered.

"No. There was no one else. Just the two of us. I guess his girlfriend will just have to find out in the newspaper."

"You have my deepest sympathies, Colonel Metzger," she told him. "If there's anything I can do, please feel free to contact me."

"Just get on with it," he told her. "I'll make the arrangements to take my brother home to New York."

"There'll be an autopsy and an investigation. It will take a few days," she answered.

"Fine."

"Colonel?" she called him back as he turned away.

"Yes, Sheriff?"

"Is there anyone who might have wanted to hurt your brother?"

"You mean kill him?" he demanded. "You're jumping to conclusions, aren't you? You haven't even done the autopsy yet."

"You said yourself he was an excellent swimmer.

His death is suspicious." She shrugged, her eyes narrowed on his sharply carved face.

His eyes glinted coldly. "Next you'll be asking me if *I* had anything to do with it!"

"Did you?"

To her surprise, he laughed instead of breaking out in an angry diatribe. "Why would I want to hurt my own brother?"

"I didn't imply that you had," she assured him.

"What else would you call that?"

"You brought it up, sir," she reminded him. "I'll be in touch when I have more information."

Sharyn trudged back to the boat ramp. Ed and Ernie were using the state kit to make imprints of tire tracks at the edge of the ramp. There was no way of knowing how many cars and trucks had been there in the past three days since the truck had disappeared. It was a long shot that they could get anything. It was a long shot that there was anything to get.

"I think this is about the best we're gonna get," Ernie told her, his face beet red in the hot sun.

"Okay. The tow truck's here. Let's go ahead and pull the truck out of the water," she decided.

"Maybe we should wait till later," Ed said with a look at the restless crowd.

"Maybe," Sharyn agreed. "But I don't like the idea of the body being down there any longer than it has to be. The sooner we get it up, the sooner we'll know what happened."

"Okay, Sheriff," Ed replied, glancing at the crowd again. "Maybe they won't even notice."

All of their faces were turned toward the plane. Sharyn had a feeling that the minute a truck was pulled out from under the lake with a dead body in it, that would change. Already some people were starting to show signs of boredom with the tedious cleaning process on the plane.

They brought in the tow truck and backed it close to the ramp. A few heads turned and a few fingers pointed as people wondered what was going on.

"Ernie, you and Ed help Joe with the crowd. Give David a call as you go. It's almost time for his shift anyway," she told him.

"We could pull the patrol cars across the police line for extra enforcement," Ernie proposed.

"Good idea." She nodded. "Let's do it."

The divers went down a last time to attach the two hooks from the towing cable to the bumper of the truck. The tow truck began to pull.

John Metzger used the ladder to climb on the side of the plane. The body was in remarkable condition, despite the years underwater. Probably protected by the mud and plant life that grew around it. The paint was still visible. Even the pilot's name was still scrolled down the side of the cockpit door.

Television reporters watched as the cockpit door was opened. The hatch slowly came up, exposing air to the inner chamber for the first time in fifty years. Cameras flashed. All eyes were glued to the pictures coming from the plane. The crowd moved closer and became quiet.

A loud Jet Ski roared by, looking at the plane that was lodged on the shore. The driver lost control of his ski when he glanced to the left of the plane and saw the red truck being slowly, inexorably, pulled from the depths of the lake, back up the same ramp it had rolled down. The ski flipped up in the air and the driver went into the lake, surfacing a moment later.

It was enough.

The crowd looked back, gaping in disbelief when they saw the back of the truck on the ramp. It was covered with mud. Water sluiced from it like a spring in the winter thaw.

Nick moved in with his team of assistants to keep Tom Metzger's body and the area in the truck around him as intact as possible as the cab came out of the water.

"Look!" someone yelled. "There's a dead guy in the truck."

While the crowd had focused on the plane, the deputies had moved the cars into position, preventing anyone from crossing the yellow tape line without crawling over them.

It was like a circus. No one knew where to look next as the plane's cockpit door was opened. The two Naval officers glanced at each other, then moved to block the view of the open cockpit.

There was a groan from the adults in the crowd and a fervent wish from the mothers who were there that they hadn't brought their young children to witness the gruesome spectacle.

"Get in there," Nick directed one of the students from the college. "We have to look at anything that washes out of the truck as it comes up."

"There's two dead guys in the plane, Mom!" one teenager reported eagerly.

"Bring the ambulance closer," Ernie said into his shoulder radio.

The truck was suspended in motion while they waited for all of the water to drain before they moved it any farther. Gloved students in white coats began to rummage through everything they found in the truck cab, marking and preserving it with plastic bags. Nick examined the body closely, speaking into a tape recorder and bagging everything he found that looked like it could be helpful.

"Everybody just stay calm," Ed said to the people as the boys in the front tried to see over the tops of the patrol cars.

"Who's the dead guy?" one boy asked.

"Looks like that guy who was workin' on the plane," another answered.

Sharyn walked to the middle of the ramp where Nick was examining the body.

"See anything unusual?"

"Nothing that would suggest foul play of any kind, although we can't be sure until we do a tox screen and take a look inside."

She nodded. "I don't see any blood on him. That must not have been blood on the cap."

"Or it washed away," he argued. "He *has* been underwater."

"Are you ready to transport him? This crowd could get too interested."

"Not quite," he replied without looking at her. "Sorry I don't have four hands and two heads! I can't know more without a closer look. The water makes time of death harder. We'll have to rely on whatever else we find."

"I understand," she answered. "Do the best you can. His brother will want answers."

"So will they." Nick nodded toward the gathering newspaper and television group. "He was pretty famous. Everyone's gonna want to know."

"I know," she agreed harshly. "One random murder

in town in the last ten years. Then I become sheriff and it's like a crime spree."

"I hardly think even a few deaths make a spree," he said quietly.

"Tell that to Ty Swindoll."

He nodded. "I'll let you know when I know something."

"Thanks."

The press were shouting questions to the deputies across the cars drawn up to the yellow lines. Sharyn told them all that she had no comment, then stepped into the patrol car and got on the phone.

The heat of the day had passed before Nick and his team were ready to move the body. There were a hundred and three bags of possible evidence. *If* there had been a crime.

From the way it looked, Sharyn considered, Tom Metzger had gone to sleep at the wheel of the truck and driven into the lake. He might have been drinking. Even a strong swimmer would have a hard time making it out of those weeds and that immediate drop-off along with the powerful suction the truck would have created as it sank into the depths of the lake.

The colonel and the two officers worked as thoroughly and patiently on the plane as Nick and his crew worked on his brother's body. Sharyn didn't think he looked toward the truck once during the long, hot afternoon, although she had to admit that there was little he could see from his vantage point.

Would she have wanted to see her sister being raised from the bottom of the lake? Probably not, she decided, looking at Tom Metzger's face.

It wasn't a pretty sight. Of course, the colonel presumably had seen far worse. Still, it was his brother. That made it different.

Sharyn was surprised to look up from her paper-work and see the colonel's face at the front window of the car.

"I'm afraid I have some bad news for you, Sheriff," he said as she climbed out of the car.

"What's that?" she wondered.

"Maybe you should come and see for yourself. I don't want to disturb the evidence any more than I already have," he said mysteriously.

"Just a minute," she said, stopping his lengthy, quick stride away from her back to the plane.

Nick was finishing up the papers and Tom Metz-ger's body was being loaded into the ambulance. The evidence was put carefully into the medical examiner's car after being tagged and labeled. Most of the students had wearily headed for home.

"Nick," she called to him. "You might want to see this."

Ernie nodded when she waved to him and followed the three of them toward the plane.

"Evidence of what?" Sharyn asked the colonel as they walked down the narrow shoreline.

Most of the crowd had thinned away during the hot-test part of the day. Now that it was cooling, people were returning to watch the two dramas unfolding. Sharyn had to alert the park service to keep onlookers away from the sites by closing down that side of the shoreline. As it was, a flotilla of boats and Jet Skis watched from about a hundred yards out on the lake. There was a half moon of orange flags on buoys that prevented any water craft from getting closer.

"The legend," John Metzger told her. "The story about this Captain Bost that brought my brother here."

"What about it?" Sharyn wondered.

"I think it might have been a cover-up."

"For what, Colonel Metzger?"

"Murder, Sheriff," he said, facing her. "Take a look in the cockpit there and tell me what you see."

This was too reminiscent of the game Nick always played with her when they had to deal with evidence of a crime. She glanced at Nick. He smirked and looked way.

Sharyn climbed carefully up the ladder that was resting alongside the body of the plane. It was wet from the water that had been fanning out across the plane all day. She pushed herself up until she could see clearly into the cockpit of the old plane.

They had cleared the weeds that had been on the inside. The bodies, little more than bones and ragged flight jackets, were sitting upright as Metzger had been in the truck.

She was closest to the navigator, who sat in the rear of the cockpit. It was pretty clear what had killed him. Impact. The whole front of his skull was caved in above the empty, staring eye sockets.

It was the pilot who was different.

His head was turned and his mouth was open. His sightless eyes bored into hers.

In the left side of his skull was a round hole. It was at the top of the bone and had clearly had been formed by something projecting from the outside to the inside of his head.

Sharyn leaned and looked at it carefully. It looked to her like Captain Bost had been shot.

"Kind of takes away from the mystery of what made

the plane crash, doesn't it?" the colonel asked from the ground.

"If someone wouldn't mind telling me what's going on," Nick interjected impatiently as Sharyn came back down the ladder.

"He was shot," she told him.

"What?" Nick demanded.

"Captain Bost was shot in the head. Take a look."

Nick climbed lithely up the ladder and stared into the front of the cockpit, leaning as close as he could to the skeletal frame of the Navy pilot.

"That's what it looks like to me," he agreed. "Nice round hole. I'd say a rifle."

"Somebody killed Billy Bost?" Ernie asked as though he couldn't believe it.

"Put a bullet through his head," the colonel confirmed. "It looks like you have two more deaths to resolve, Sheriff."

Sharyn glanced up at Nick, who shook his head wearily.

"I'll get my bag."

Chapter Four

Sharyn waited impatiently at the office for the results of the preliminary autopsy on Tom Metzger. She
would have to wait a lot longer for results of the tests
on Captain Billy Bost and his copilot. She didn't mind.
She wasn't anxious to put herself in the way of a legend.

She had a summons from the county commission.
They would be having a televised meeting Tuesday
night and "requested" her presence to clear up a few
details.

"Sounds like trouble, Sheriff," Ed told her when he
saw the summons.

"Never mind," she said, folding the letter. "I want
the two of you out on the lake today. Talk to as many
people as you can. We canvassed the shore and no
one saw anything. Maybe we'll have better luck with
boaters and fishermen."

"We don't even know it's a homicide," Joe protested.

She nodded. "You're right. But we would like to know what happened, even if the death is ruled accidental. So get moving."

Ernie was laying out all the information he could dig up on Billy Bost and his historic flight across Palmer Lake.

"Is Nick sure that had to be a bullet hole?" he wondered. "I mean, the man was underwater for a long time."

"It looked like a bullet hole to everyone who saw it. We won't know until the end of the week. Nick sent the skull to the forensics lab in Raleigh."

"There's a professor at UNCC that does that stuff too," Ernie told her. "I read about her in the paper."

"Well, if Raleigh doesn't have the answer, I guess we can try the professor," Sharyn answered. "In the meantime, we're going to believe that it is a bullet hole and find as much information as we can about Captain Bost." She put her chin in her hand, leaning on her desk. "You know, I really thought he was just a legend."

Ernie shook his head. "I remember folks talking about it when I was a young 'un. I used to look out over the lake and think about Billy Bost being under there. We used to tell ghost stories and scare ourselves silly when we camped out at night. You know, the ghost of Captain Billy coming out of the lake to get people? All dripping with water and slime."

Sharyn shuddered. "I get the idea. But what's the reality, Ernie? What really happened?"

"According to the old *Palmer Mountain Gazette,* he was flying low to impress his sweetheart because the Navy said there wasn't time for them to meet. He dipped his wings and lost control of the plane. It crashed into the lake. They sent out some divers to try to find the plane but they couldn't locate it." He shrugged and touched his graying mustache. "I guess they needed the new equipment to do it."

"How do you think Tom Metzger found out about the story?" she asked, twirling her pencil. "Something or someone had to make him think it was real."

"I only found a small mention of Metzger coming to town to look for the plane," he told her. "Obviously Jimmy Dalton down at the *Gazette* wasn't too impressed with the idea."

"No," she agreed. "He just likes publishing stuff about me."

Ernie grinned. "You're more interesting, Sheriff. Besides, who would've thought they'd really find the plane?"

"Someone might have."

Ernie shook his head. "You mean someone didn't want him to find it?"

"I don't know, Ernie," she admitted. "Let's be prepared. But I don't want you to do the legwork. Pass this off to one of the college kids. I'd like you to stay on our present-day problem. Let's find out what we can about Tom Metzger."

"And his brother?" he asked hopefully.

She nodded. "Definitely."

"I'll dig around some more," he promised. "I could go down and talk to Jimmy at the *Gazette*. See what he remembers."

"That sounds good. I have Ed and Joe out on the lake. I'm not calling David in unless we need him. He's like working with a bear."

Ernie laughed. "The whole business of trying to impress a woman is too much like work."

"Is that why you never married?" she wondered absently.

"Something like that, Sheriff," he agreed, then got up. "You could say the example I had growing up didn't impress me too much. I'm gonna stroll over and have a talk with Jimmy."

Sharyn watched him leave, trying to recall what little she could about Ernie's family. She remembered that his father had been in prison and that his mother had died young. But she couldn't remember much else.

She looked over the newspaper files on her desk. Billy Bost was twenty-one years old that day more than fifty years before when his plane had plunged into the cold, dark water. The military had ruled the accident pilot error. It seemed Billy Bost had come some twenty-five miles off his course to signal his girlfriend. The military found this disturbing, and even without finding the plane, decided Billy had been reckless.

The paper named his parents. Subsequent days later, when the investigation was closed and sealed under military jurisdiction because it happened during wartime, they announced a memorial service for him. But they never said who his sweetheart was or if it was true that she had thrown herself into the lake and drowned. The second man in the plane was Captain Joe Walsh from Philadelphia.

The Navy estimated that the plane went down in about 140 feet of water. There had been a map of the crash site but it had been lost down through the years. Tom Metzger had gone by descriptions from people who had witnessed the crash. Billy's parents were dead but his brother was still alive. Sharyn put her calls on hold and took a patrol car out to Bobby Bost's place.

Bobby still lived in the house he and his only brother had grown up in. It was a two-story white clapboard that sat in an alcove of the lake. If they had been outside, Sharyn realized, they would have seen Billy crash into the lake. The plane had been found close by.

Bobby was ten years younger than his brother. He opened the door and welcomed Sharyn warmly when she arrived.

"You're here about Billy, aren't you?" he asked with a smile as he showed her into the living room.

Sharyn sat down on one of the olive-green chairs while Bobby's wife, Macy, went to get some iced tea. "Yes, I am," she answered. "You're not surprised."

The sheriff's office had not made it public knowledge yet that the pilot had been shot. She had expected him to be loaded with questions.

"Well, I knew they pulled up the plane. I didn't watch. But I heard about it."

"And you thought I might be interested in talking to you?"

He nodded as Macy brought back the iced tea in tall glasses. Already a film of condensation had developed on the outside of the glasses. Macy hurried back for napkins.

He nodded. He was a tall, heavyset man with a full head of gray hair. His blue eyes were certain when they looked at her.

"There's not a lot of us left who were there that day, Sheriff. Besides, I've always known Billy was killed. I thought someone might investigate now."

Sharyn thanked Macy for the tea and the napkin. "Killed?"

"As sure as I'm sitting here with you. We all knew it back then."

"There's no report of it in the paper," she commented.

"Of course not!" He shrugged. "Those G-men would've never let us say anything like that. It was all closed up and decided on. Pilot error!" He hooted and slapped his knee. "Billy had flown five hundred hours in a plane like that one, Sheriff. He had flown hundreds of missions. He knew what he was doing. He was a good pilot."

"And you told the military this?" she asked, taking out her notebook.

"They knew it already. There was no point repeating it for them."

"Did you see the crash, Bobby?" she wondered.

"I did. So did my parents."

"Can you describe it for me?"

His blue eyes took on a faraway look. "We were inside. Pa was getting ready to go fishing. I was home sick that day. It was real quiet back then. You know, we didn't have motorboats on the lake and planes didn't fly over a lot. There weren't many cars out here. Billy's plane flew down so close that it made the windows rattle. We heard him coming a mile away."

"What happened then, Bobby?" she asked.

"Well, we went outside to see if we could see the plane."

"You knew it was him?"

"He'd told us he was gonna fly low and dip his wings to Mary Sue."

"Mary Sue?"

"His girlfriend. Well, more than that. They were gonna be married when he came home."

"Okay. So you went outside?"

"Yeah, we went outside and the plane flew right over our heads. It looked like it was so low, I could have reached up and touched it. There were people watching it from all over town. Everybody was looking up in the air at Billy's plane."

"So, everyone knew he was coming home that day?"

Bobby laughed. "He was my big brother and I loved him. He was a hero in this town, Sheriff. We were all proud of him. We followed his career like some people followed the adventure movies. And he loved it. Billy always wanted to be a star."

"So his plane went by overhead?"

"It went over us and Ma waved and waved. We didn't know if he could see us or not. She swore she could see him in his goggles and his leather jacket wearing his lucky scarf. He went over us and got to the middle of the lake. He dipped his wing but he didn't touch the water."

"Then what happened?" Sharyn wondered.

"It was like the plane choked and fell. Billy didn't lose control of it. We could see him fighting to hold on to the stick."

"You could see Billy through the cockpit glass?"

"Pa did. Ma was crying. The plane went under before any of us could move. Sank like a stone."

"So, that's why you thought Billy was killed?"

"That's why. I swear to this day somebody killed him."

"Any idea who would have done that?" Sharyn questioned, thinking it might be a start.

"No one in this town," he replied staunchly. "Everyone here loved Billy. I think it was a Nazi sympathizer. They found out Billy's route and followed him here. Probably from Charlotte." He spat out the town's name like a curse.

"Did you call Tom Metzger about this?" she asked him.

"No, that wasn't my doing. He did come talk to me before he started all that stuff looking for the plane. He had me take him down to the lake and show him where I thought the plane crashed."

"And what about Billy's sweetheart? Is she still alive?"

"Mary Sue? Sure. She lives right next door. That's how Billy and her got to be so close. They grew up together. She got married and had some kids but she stayed in her mother's house."

Sharyn closed her book. "I appreciate your help, Bobby."

"No problem, Sheriff. If I can tell you anything else, just come on by."

"Thanks. I'll let you know about Billy."

"Thanks, Sheriff. You know, me and Macy voted for you. Your daddy did a good job here and you're just like him."

"Thanks, Bobby. Macy," she acknowledged the quiet little woman who nodded her head like a bird.

Sharyn sat in the patrol car and looked out over the lake, imagining what it must have been like for Billy's family to watch their hero son die in that terrible crash. The chances were Mary Sue had run outside to see her tribute too. They had all stood by, helplessly, while Billy had fallen to his death.

She rang the bell and knocked at the white clapboard house next to the Bosts' home but there was no answer. There was no car in the drive. She'd have to come back.

Mary Sue had married, apparently, and forgotten her pilot sweetheart. She'd gone on with her life and had children and probably grandchildren. That was life, Sharyn supposed.

Ernie called her on the car phone to let her know that he was back from his interview with Jimmy Dalton. Sharyn started the car engine and headed back to the office.

Billy Bost's plane was surrounded by a high fence to keep away the sightseers. It was a few hundred feet down the shore from where Bobby described it falling into the lake. It was strange to think that the plane had hidden that secret for fifty years, yet Bobby claimed to have known for that long that the pilot-error theory wasn't true.

Why hadn't the military investigated more thoroughly? she wondered. Was a verdict of pilot error better than finding the truth?

Captain Parker and Lt. Wilkes approached her on the steps to the office.

"Hello, Sheriff. Could we have a moment of your time?"

"Of course," Sharyn answered, noting that they were both in uniform. "Come inside."

She told Trudy to hold her calls, then ushered the officers inside. Lt. Wilkes closed the door, then took a seat.

"What can I do for you?" Sharyn wondered.

"We were wondering about the Navy pilots," Captain Parker said quickly. "When will their remains be released? The Navy will be burying them with full military honors."

"It will be a few days at least. Maybe longer. It takes a specialist to find out information about what little was left of them," Sharyn explained, getting curious.

"We could take care of that for you," Lt. Wilkes offered. "The Navy would be happy to foot the bill for their autopsies."

Sharyn studied them closely. There was something more there. "I appreciate the offer, Captain, Lieutenant. But the state frowns on that sort of thing."

"Both men were technically military property at the time of their deaths, Sheriff," Lt. Wilkes told her curtly.

"That was over fifty years ago," Sharyn reminded them. "We could take it to court, I suppose, to see what the jurisdiction is on the case."

"That's not necessary," Captain Parker said quickly. She stood and nodded to Sharyn. "If you could let us know when we can plan the burials?"

"Of course."

"What was that all about?" Ernie asked, watching the two officers leave.

"I'm not really sure," Sharyn admitted. "But the Navy is still interested in Billy Bost's accident."

"Maybe they were afraid Nazis were sabotaging their planes," Ernie said. "Jimmy Dalton told me that was the popular theory after the plane went down."

"Billy's brother thought the same thing." She explained the whole interview with Bobby Bost.

"Maybe they were afraid people would panic," Ernie suggested. "Jimmy Dalton was just a kid when it happened. I guess around the same age as Bobby Bost.

He barely remembers it but he didn't see it, either. He was in town at the elementary school."

"It was before the big school was built on the lake?" she asked.

"Guess so." Ernie shrugged. "It was back quite a bit, Sheriff. Even if someone did shoot Billy Bost, what are the chances we'll ever find who did it? Most of the witnesses are probably dead or really old by this time."

"Mary Sue is still alive."

"Mary Sue?"

"Billy's girlfriend. She didn't throw herself into the lake."

"You think Mary Sue shot Billy?" Ernie wondered in disbelief.

"No. I think she might be able to tell us something more about it."

"As far as Jimmy is concerned, no one in this town would have done anything to hurt Billy. Everyone loved him. He was like Superman."

"That's why Bobby said it had to be Nazis," she recounted. "No one else would have done anything to Billy."

"Maybe that won't be a bullet hole," Ernie contemplated. "I'd rather not investigate a murder that happened when I was a baby."

"I know what you mean, Ernie," she agreed, packing up her files. She zipped them into a bag and slung it on her shoulder. "I hope it isn't a bullet hole, but we both know what that report is going to say when it comes back."

Ernie frowned. "I'll just wait and be surprised, if it's okay with you, Sheriff."

"Got anything yet on either Metzger brother?"

"Just the usual so far. No arrest records. Neither one was ever in prison. I should have more back by morning."

They walked to the courthouse where the commission meetings were held on the first Tuesday of every month. There were a few reporters talking with commissioners in the hall but they ignored the sheriff. It wasn't unusual for Sharyn to be there. She reported to the commission every month. It had been unusual for them to summon her.

A few commissioners nodded to her and Ernie as they took their seats in the large, chair-filled room. The commission members filtered in slowly as the hour neared for the meeting. Ty Swindoll was the last to arrive, with a tornado-like flourish and a bevy of apologies for being there so close to the hour.

Sharyn looked at her report that consisted of what had happened during the month. It was a detailed account of the office expenses and her operating procedures. She knew she wasn't here for the normal meeting, however. Ty Swindoll was going to rake her over the coals about the helicopter trip. She felt his beady little blue eyes staring at her but she didn't look up.

Nick came into the room and sat down beside her. Ernie looked up and nodded at him.

"What are you doing here?" she whispered.

"I knew you'd want to know right away about Metzger," he told her. "I called your office but you were already gone."

"This might not be the best time," she informed him tautly as the head commissioner brought the meeting to order.

"Our usual agenda for tonight is put on hold to find

answers to some more serious allegations against the sheriff's department," the head commissioner told the audience. "Mr. Swindoll, if you'd like to take the floor.' "

"Thanks, Reed."

As Ty Swindoll bemoaned the sheriff department's budget and the lack of adequate green space being bought for the county, Nick filled Sharyn in on the Metzger autopsy.

"We have Sheriff Howard here today to answer some very important questions about the new helicopter that was purchased at outrageous cost to the county for the sheriff's department," Ty Swindoll concluded, staring out into the audience.

Sharyn and Nick sat with their heads close together, talking about the autopsy. Ernie cleared his throat and tapped Sharyn on the shoulder.

"Sheriff Howard?" Ty Swindoll called her name. "Can you explain why it was necessary to take the helicopter out when there was no emergency, no lost child to find? Just a need for you to come home from your camping trip?"

Sharyn stood up slowly, handing Ernie her briefcase full of papers.

"A man was missing and may have been murdered, Mr. Swindoll. That seemed to be enough of an emergency for me."

The word murder was repeated through the courthouse, bringing heads up and tape recorders out.

"Murdered?" Ty looked to his contemporaries. "Why weren't we informed?"

"Because that's the sheriff's department business. To find out when a crime has been committed and investigate."

Ty adjusted his tie and glanced down at his papers. "Well, Sheriff Howard, why were you in the mountains at a time like this?"

"Obviously because there was no way for me to know it was a time like this before it happened, Commissioner. I haven't had a single day off in over two years. I thought I might be able to go hiking in the mountains for a few days. In fact, if you'll check your records, the commission ordered me to take my vacation time so that it didn't accrue."

Reed Harker, head of the commission, nodded. "That is true, Ty. We told her to take her vacation time."

"But not during a murder investigation!"

"If I may," Nick said, standing on Sharyn's left side.

"And you are?" Ty asked.

"Nick Thomopolis, the county medical examiner," he introduced himself.

"Proceed, Mr. Thomopolis," Reed declared.

"The investigation into Tom Metzger's disappearance only began a few days ago. The results from his autopsy were just finalized today. There was no way anyone could have known there was a murder."

"Including the sheriff's deputies?" Ty pounced on his words.

Sharyn interrupted. "My deputies did what they thought was best. The investigation was under way into what had happened to Mr. Metzger. There was some evidence that there might have been foul play. They made the decision that it was important for me to be here. I support their decision."

"Then who pays the one thousand one hundred eighty-two dollars it costs every time that helicopter goes up?" Ty asked. "The state won't, even though it was their law that we had to have it. Would you like to pay that cost, Sheriff?"

Sharyn frowned. "I don't think it was in the state's charter or mandate to charge for the usage of the helicopter, Commissioner."

"That may be true," Swindoll continued. "But we don't want to pay for pleasure jaunts by county officials. I don't think *that* was part of the deal, either."

"This was not a pleasure jaunt, Commissioner," Sharyn argued strongly. "This was a decision made by the sheriff's department for the good of the community. This helicopter is a piece of equipment just like a patrol car or an ambulance. I don't see any reason to question its use in this instance. I'm sure the commission doesn't want the sheriff's department deciding where funding is coming from before we dispatch an ambulance or a patrol car in an emergency."

There were a few moments of quiet but heated debate among the commission before Ty Swindoll sat forward in his chair again to use the microphone. His face was an unhealthy shade of red. "I'd like to move that the commissioners approve the helicopter going up from now on, before it takes off."

Sharyn smiled. "Wouldn't that defeat the purpose of having an emergency helicopter, sir? The helicopter wasn't bought just for the sheriff department's use. It was also purchased as an emergency medical evacuation system. Does someone from the commission want to be responsible for the time it takes to get permission, even if it costs someone their life?"

The commissioners whispered among themselves. Ty was sweating profusely and his voice was a little louder than the others.

"We'll leave that jurisdiction to you for now, Sheriff," Reed Harker said quietly when they had finished.

"Then I propose we take up the argument that Diamond Springs doesn't need as many people in the sheriff's office as we have right now," Ty was quick to add. His thin face and thinning hair made his eyes intense as he glared at Sharyn.

"Let me make this completely clear," Sharyn replied calmly in a voice of deadly seriousness. "I won't be responsible for a sheriff's office with less manpower. The county is growing, which I think is your usual argument, Mr. Swindoll. We barely have the officers to handle the growth as it is. You want a good place to raise your children? You want your homes kept safe? Then you can't decrease the department. If anything, we need to add a few deputies. We're strained to handle the outlying areas and the town."

The commissioners whispered between themselves again. Ernie nodded at Sharyn with a thumbs-up. Nick smiled and watched the five men and three women at the long table.

"We take your point, Sheriff," Reed Harker told her. He had been on the commission for fifteen years. He had seen the changes in the area and he knew the problems they were having keeping up with the outlying growth spurt along the interstate highway.

"There won't be any cutbacks in the sheriff's department for now and we will take under advisement the request for more officers. As for the helicopter ride, I think we can all agree that this, uh, situation warranted the sheriff's immediate attention. However, we will be asking that a log be kept on helicopter usage in the future."

Sharyn nodded. "Thank you, sir."

"You're doing a fine job, Sheriff," Betty Fontana, another commissioner, praised her.

"Thank you, ma'am. I do the best I can."

"And this is no way a reflection of our esteem for you, Sheriff," Charlie Sommers assured her. Sharyn Howard had found his daughter's killer and brought him to justice. He would never forget.

"Thank you, Mr. Sommers."

"Can we move on now?" Ty Swindoll demanded. "You're excused, Sheriff." He waved his hand toward her.

"Run along, run along," Ernie whispered from the side of his mouth as they walked out of the room.

"The man's an idiot," Nick said hotly.

"But he's effective," Sharyn replied, letting the door close behind them.

"Everyone's scared to look at him the wrong way," Ernie explained. "I don't understand it."

"I think they're afraid the people from outside the city will rise up in their SUVs and take over," Sharyn told him.

"How could you stand there and take that?" Nick wondered, looking at her.

"It's part of my job," she said. "Bureaucracy. I heard my father complain about it every time he had to meet with them."

"But Swindoll was wrong!" Nick continued as they walked back to the sheriff's office. "It's not fair for you to defend your actions to him. The man's a jerk!"

"I agree with Nick," Ernie stated for the record, though his voice was a little less vehement.

"That's fine," Sharyn told them both. "I appreciate your support. But there's only one other answer— backing down. And I won't give him that satisfaction."

Ernie shrugged and put his hands in his pockets.

Nick loosened his tie and took a deep breath.

"I appreciate you coming over there, Nick," she said to him. "Joe and Ed should be back by now. I'd like them to hear what you have to say about the autopsy."

He nodded. "Good. Let's get this over with."

Ed and Joe took their coffee into the interrogation room with Ernie and Nick. Sharyn grabbed a Coke while Trudy told her what messages had come in while she was gone. There was a message from Mary Sue Anderson. She wanted to speak with her as soon as possible.

"I think that's going to be tomorrow," Sharyn said to Trudy. "What are you still doing here?"

"I'm on my way out now," Trudy told her. "Don't worry, I'm already off the clock."

Sharyn's mouth tightened. The whole department was worried about cutting back when taxes were up and the county was doing well for itself. It made her angry that they were being hit hardest for the money the commission wanted to spend on other things. It especially made her angry to see her people work for free.

There wasn't anything she could do about it. At least not then. But she would be looking for the right moment for that battle.

She took her Coke and headed for the interrogation room. Nick, Ernie, Joe, and Ed were talking intently across the scarred wooden table. Until she walked into the room. Conversation shut down like a power switch had been thrown.

"Problems?" she wondered as she took her place at the table.

"Not a thing, Sheriff," Ed assured her.

"Everything's fine, Sheriff," Nick repeated.

"Good." She glanced around the room at the men's faces. As ususal Ed was sporting his pretty-boy look with his blue eyes wide open. Joe was dark and thin lipped, not giving away anything. Ernie nodded and smiled. She *knew* he was hiding something. And Nick . . .

Well, who knew what Nick was thinking?

"Okay, if Nick hasn't already told you, preliminary autopsy results on Mr. Metzger don't look good. Nick?"

Nick took out his reports. "Mr. Metzger died late Sunday night. There was no sign of struggle. No sign of him having been injured in any way. No marks around the head or neck. There was something in the tox screen, though, that made me suspicious. He had a huge amount of sleeping pills in him."

"Barbiturates?" Ed wondered.

"No, this is over-the-counter stuff. We're still trying to isolate the brand but we should have that soon."

"Maybe he was just tired and needed a good night's sleep," Ernie suggested.

"When I did the autopsy, I found that he was alive when he went into the water. Technically, he drowned. But he also had possibly a bottle of this stuff in him. More than someone would take for a good night's sleep."

"Suicide?" Joe threw out on the table.

"I don't know," Nick admitted. "I suppose he could have swallowed the pills, then climbed in his truck and waited to feel sleepy so he could drive into the lake."

"Would the pills have killed him on their own?" Sharyn wondered.

"Possibly," Nick answered uncertainly. "I'd say,

probably not. He was in good health, no obvious medical problems. The chances are he would have slept for a long time. If he had gone to the hospital they would have pumped his stomach, but it wasn't a matter of life and death."

"Probably," Joe tacked on.

"Probably," Nick agreed.

Sharyn sighed. "It's not unusual for a person intent on suicide to use two different forms of doing away with themselves. Maybe that's all this was."

"Maybe," Joe said. "Do we know anything about him? Was he prone to suicide? Was something bad happening in his life?"

"His brother mentioned a woman," Sharyn told them. "He said he was involved with a new woman but that he hadn't met her. Ernie's looking into his personal life. And his brother's."

They all sat quietly for a moment, thinking about Tom Metzger.

"So, do we rule this a suicide?" Ernie asked of the room in general.

"What about the truck?" Ed asked. "Anything on the truck?"

"Not yet," Nick answered. "I checked this afternoon."

Sharyn looked at the picture of Tom Metzger that was laid out before her on the table. "Let's hold off until we get everything else together. Can you do that?" she asked Nick.

He nodded. "I feel inconclusive about this anyway. It could have been suicide, I guess. But it could have been something else."

"You mean you really think someone murdered him by putting sleeping pills into his drink or something, then putting him in the truck and letting it roll down the ramp into the lake?" Ernie queried, his eyes narrowed on Nick's dark face.

"My Sicilian grandmother always told me that sometimes you have to see the whole picture to know the truth about something." Nick shrugged. "I don't feel like we're seeing the whole picture."

"What could the whole picture be?" Ed asked.

"Well, I'm pretty sure we're going to find out that Captain Billy Bost was murdered fifty years ago," he explained. "What if whoever murdered the heroic captain didn't want anyone to find out about it? It's been a mystery all these years. Everyone thought the plane just went down. What if the same person who murdered Captain Bost murdered Tom Metzger to keep their secret?"

Chapter Five

"When was the last time you talked to your brother?" Sharyn asked as Col. Metzger worked on the twin-engine bomber that was starting to gleam in the summer sun.

"I talked to him on the phone before I came up here," the colonel replied as he cleaned fifty years of silt from the plane. The two Naval officers were close by, giving Sharyn the impression that they were listening to the conversation.

"Did he seem like he was in good spirits?"

"As good as ever. Better, maybe. He seemed to be quite taken with his new companion."

"But you have no idea who this woman was?"

"Not at all," the colonel told her. "I explained that situation to you, Sheriff."

"I remember," Sharyn replied quickly. "But the woman might be able to shed some light on what happened to your brother."

76

"You mean taking sleeping pills and rolling his truck down the ramp?" John Metzger stopped cleaning and looked down at her.

She looked up at him. "That's what I mean, Colonel."

"You know, in this light, your hair is on fire," he said intently. He went back to cleaning the plane. "Call me John, Sheriff. I'll call you Sharyn. In private, of course. I wouldn't want to demean you in public."

The headlines of the *Gazette* that morning had been a reprint of the picture of Sharyn in her sweatpants running from the helicopter with the story about Swindoll asking her to pay for the use of the machine. And her refusal. She had steadfastly refused to take any calls on it before she left the office that morning.

Sharyn shrugged off the colonel's very personal remarks. "Do you think your brother would commit suicide?"

"That might not be the best question to ask me, Sharyn," he replied candidly. "After all, I'm probably the only one in his will. Naturally, I wouldn't want his life insurance to be messed up with the idea of suicide."

She narrowed her eyes as she looked at him in the sun. "Are you, Colonel?"

"John, please. The only one in his will?"

"Yes."

"Not that I'm aware of, although I am his only living relative. He probably left it all to a young writers' group or some spotted owl in Timbuktu."

"You haven't seen his will, then?"

"No."

"Do you think this woman could be in it?"

"I couldn't say, although he would have had to

change it recently. He's only known her a short while."

"You knew a lot about the relationship not to have met her," Sharyn said.

John Metzger jumped down from the plane, landing right at Sharyn's feet, then bringing himself up to his full height, which was several inches taller than her.

"I know what he told me. It was a game, Sharyn. He wanted to tell me what I was missing, what I couldn't have. He was afraid to tell me any details like her name. He was afraid to introduce me. But if you're asking me if my brother committed suicide, I'd say no. Could he have been careless, sloppy in what he was doing, and an accident happened? Definitely. Talk to anyone. My brother was no perfectionist."

Sharyn took a deep breath but didn't move back even though John Metzger was nearly in her face. She could see the dark lines where he'd shaved that morning, the tight skin around his hard eyes and cruel mouth.

"So, you think he made a mistake? Took too many pills, didn't judge their efficacy, and got in his truck. The rest just happened?"

"That's what I think. What do you think, Sharyn?"

She stared into his unforgiving face. "I think you had a very low opinion of your brother. He was a Pulitzer Prize winner, a brilliant author, lecturer, and archaeologist."

"All of those things mean nothing," he ground out savagely, walking away from her abruptly. "He was only skin-deep, Sharyn. All glory, no guts. He wrote about other people's lives that he could never have because he was a coward."

"Do you know how he found out about the plane in the lake?" she asked him, changing tactics.

He shrugged. "I don't know. He had his sources, I suppose. He just called me to do the work on it. Give him the details about the plane."

"But as far as you know, everything in his life was all right?"

He bit off the end of a cigar and spat it on the ground. "As far as I know, he was rich, healthy, and stupid enough not to care how he got there. Now, I get to ask you a question, Sharyn."

"All right," she replied, putting away her notebook.

"What about you? What made you become sheriff of this backwater? You're an attractive young woman. Why aren't you home having babies and cooking supper?"

She frowned. "I took over the office from my father. He was killed at the convenience store at the edge of the county line. Someday, I might be home having babies and cooking supper. Right now, I'm trying to find out what happened to your brother."

He took a step toward her again. "Have dinner with me tonight."

It was more a command than an offer.

"I'm afraid I'm busy," she replied solidly. "But thanks."

He took her hand in his. "You and I could be good together, Sharyn. I know you must feel it."

"Sheriff?" Ernie came up behind her. "We've been calling you. I came out because there wasn't an answer. Everything okay?"

Ernie glared at the colonel like a terrier growling at a Great Dane.

"Everything's fine," Sharyn told him, deftly removing her hand from the colonel's. "I'll be in contact to let you know what the medical examiner decides is the cause of death."

"And what about us?" he retorted.

"I appreciate the offer, sir," she told him. "This isn't a good time."

Ernie walked with her down the lakeshore toward the patrol cars parked near the ramp.

"I can't believe you'd . . . seriously . . ."

"Ernie," she reassured him. "I wouldn't . . . seriously."

He took a deep breath. "That's good. Your poor daddy—"

"—would know better than to try to tell me who to date, Ernie," she said firmly. "What brings you out here?"

"Nick called. He wanted us to come down to the hospital. He thinks he has something. And I have everything you've ever wanted to know about the Metzger brothers." He held a thick file up for her to see it and waggled his eyebrows. "It's pretty juicy!"

She nodded. "Okay. Let's take your car."

Sharyn looked through the file while Ernie hit the highlights.

"Colonel Metzger wasn't kidding about their relationship. From what I can gather, it wasn't unusual for them to insult each other publicly. Tom Metzger even walked into a restaurant and took a swing at his brother two years ago. As you can see from the newspaper clippings, they're famous for their feuding."

She turned the copy of the newspaper clipping sideways and saw the picture of Tom Metzger angrily assaulting his brother. There was also an article about the colonel claiming that his brother took some information from his memoirs without his consent. It never went further than an accusation.

"Either brother ever married?" Sharyn wondered. "Have any children?"

"Tom was never married. No children that I could find record of," Ernie replied as he drove through the sun-baked streets. "John, however, married a woman five years ago. No children. Nothing unusual. No press photos except for the wedding announcement. They both look like gargoyles in that."

"Joanna Powers, twenty-eight," Sharyn read out loud, then glanced at Ernie. "No help here. What a terrible picture!"

Ernie shrugged. "I could contact her family. They must have a better one."

"I'd like to talk to her. She might have known what was going on between the brothers better than anyone else. And she might have known Tom's girlfriend. Let's find her," she suggested, then continued. "No money problems for either man. Just the personal feud between them."

"It's awfully public for either brother to make a move against the other," Ernie concluded. "And all the incidents of violence were attributed to Tom."

"Unless one of them thought they had the perfect cover," Sharyn concluded as they reached the hospital.

Diamond Springs County Hospital was a huge red brick fortress of a building. The medical examiner had his offices in the basement, where the bomb shelter used to be, along with the morgue. It was a dark place where overhead fluorescent lights glared down like baleful eyes on the sterile sheets and pale bodies.

Nick was teaching a class when they arrived. A dead man lay on a table between him and his group of five students. Three of them looked queasy. The other two weren't looking at the cadaver.

"This place gives me the creeps." Ernie said softly.

"It's the basement," she replied, equally hushed. "It feels like the whole building is on top of you."

Ernie smirked. "I think it's the dead bodies, Sheriff."

Sharyn looked at him. "If I order you to call me Sharyn, at least when we're alone, would that make any difference?"

"None at all," he responded.

"You called my father by his given name," she argued. "Why can't you call me Sharyn?"

"Your father was a different story," he told her. "I'd known him most of my life. We were friends."

"Aren't we friends?" she debated.

"Not the same way."

"You're a stubborn mule, Ernie," she said finally.

"Thank you, Sheriff."

"You took your time getting here," Nick said when he had finished the class. He discarded his gloves and gown in the trash.

"The sheriff was out questioning the colonel," Ernie explained. "I had to go and get her."

"Alone?" he began, looking at her.

"Don't start," she returned. "What have you got?"

He glared at her. "It's more what I don't got."

"Speak English," she requested.

"I've gone over everything we found at his motel and at his work area near the site. I went over everything in the truck. There's nothing."

"Nothing?" Ernie asked.

"No prints. It's like everything has been wiped clean. Metzger didn't leave any prints. Not on his bathroom glass. Not on the doorknob. Everything was clean."

"Maybe he was a clean fanatic," Sharyn suggested.

"And something's missing," Nick continued.

"What?"

"The bottle of sleeping pills. He couldn't have taken the pills at his motel, then driven to the site. They would have worked too quickly. He had to take them at the site. I suspect in a cup of coffee. When he climbed in his truck, he would have been out of it."

"Let me see that inventory list David gave us of his belongings, Ernie," Sharyn said.

When they looked, there was no listing for a bottle, empty or otherwise, of sleeping pills.

"He wouldn't have had time to run off with them somewhere," Nick argued. "He wouldn't have dropped them in the trash or in the truck. Maybe on the ground between the two. He certainly wouldn't have had time to wipe everything down."

Ernie shrugged. "If he was out of it, he could have dropped the bottle on the ground. Someone could have picked it up before we got there to look for him."

"The site was wiped clean too, Ernie," Nick told him. "There were no prints on the coffee mug at the site. It was wiped clean, inside and out. I think the pills were given to him in his coffee."

"And the murderer wiped down the cup after he was done?"

"I sent the cup away to an independent lab where a friend of mine works. We should know tomorrow but I'm willing to bet that there will be residue in there. Coffee and sleeping pills."

"It's thin," Sharyn told him doubtfully. "Very thin."

"What about the cup?"

"If the cup comes back the way you suspect," she promised, "we'll take a look at it. Are you going for a homicide?"

Nick nodded. The fluorescent light caught on the silver strands in his black hair, making his dark eyes look shadowed. "That's what I want."

She glanced at her watch. "Thanks, Nick. Let me know if you have anything else."

When they walked out of the hospital into the hot summer sun, Ernie whistled and shook his head. "You know, this is so thin, you can see through it."

"I know." She got into the car. "There's a lot of variables."

"Even if the cup comes back and there is residue in it, he could have done it himself. My mother always crushed up pills in her food and drink to take them. He might have done the same."

"And the missing bottle could be anywhere."

"And as for no prints." Ernie started the car and looked for traffic.

"That is unusual," Sharyn answered. "Find the colonel's wife, then see if you can find out who's settling Tom Metzger's estate. Even the cleanest people in the world don't wipe off their fingerprints!"

"You think someone could have killed him for his money?" he asked, his thin, expressive face astonished.

"I think anything is possible. But we need to find out who Tom's new woman is, Ernie."

When they walked into the office, Trudy told her that she had a call on her line from Evan Goldblum.

"Sheriff Harwood," the attorney enunciated on the phone. "I'm Evan Goldblum, Tom Metzger's attorney."

"That's Sheriff *Howard,* and I'm glad you called, Mr. Goldblum," Sharyn corrected. "We're investigating your client's death and we're going to need some information."

"Is there some problem, Sheriff?"

"We aren't sure yet," she answered calmly. "That's why we're investigating. I do need to ask you one question."

"If I can answer," the lawyer replied.

"Who stands to benefit from Mr. Metzger's death?"

"I'm afraid that's somewhere in lawyer/client privilege right now," he answered quickly.

"I'd hate to have to issue a subpoena to bring you down here and testify before a grand jury," she added slyly. "It's a hundred degrees in the shade."

"Since it will be a matter of public record shortly," he decided quickly, "I can tell you that it's the Metzger School of Writing. He wanted everything to go to keeping good writers out there working."

"Nothing to his brother?"

"No, there are no personal bequests," the lawyer told her. "You think Tom was killed?"

"We aren't sure yet, sir. We're waiting for more evidence. Do you have any theories that might be helpful?"

"Tom was an easy man to like, Sheriff. And a hard man to ignore. As far as I know, he didn't have an enemy in the world. And if he did, I can't imagine them going out there to kill him. Only a handful of people knew he was there."

"What handful would that be exactly?" she queried.

"Well, I only found out yesterday that Tom was going down there. Tom's agent and his editor knew, I'm sure. That's probably all. Tom was pretty tightlipped, especially on a project. He was a very private man by nature."

"We've questioned if it could be a possible suicide," she stated.

"Suicide? Tom wasn't the type. He certainly wasn't despondent. He had a great life."

"What about his new girlfriend?"

"Which one? Tom was always with a different woman. He had been keeping company with a particular woman lately, I guess. Maybe the last six months or so. They seemed serious."

"Do you know who she was?"

"Nope, sorry. He was keeping their relationship a secret. He was a *very* private man, Sheriff. I think she might have been married. The only time I saw her, they were going away somewhere."

Sharyn pounced on the obvious. "What makes you think she was married?"

"I don't know," he admitted. "Just some things that Tom said to me."

"And you never recall hearing even her first name, Mr. Goldblum?" she wondered.

"Not even a nickname. Sorry." The lawyer asked to be kept informed. Sharyn agreed, then hung up the phone. She stared for a long time at her desktop.

Well, no one would have killed Tom Metzger for his money, she considered. Unless it was someone at the school, which seemed far-fetched.

No one knew of anything personal against him that might make someone want to kill him. Not a lot of people even knew that he was in Diamond Springs. Of those people, his agent was out of the country. His publisher was in New York. His brother was on the road from D.C. Only the girlfriend was missing from the puzzle.

If Tom Metzger *was* killed, it seemed likely the theory about Captain Bost's murderer might make sense. If the person who shot Captain Bost and caused co-pilot Joe Walsh's death over fifty years ago was still alive, it was possible that he or she could have killed to keep the world from discovering it.

She didn't like the theory. She really didn't like the idea of investigating a triple murder, especially one from fifty years earlier. But she might end up with no choice in the matter.

Sharyn and Ernie went out after lunch to talk to the owner of the motel where Tom Metzger had been staying. He opened the door to the room for them and assured them that no one had touched it since the deputy had visited him when Metzger was missing.

Everything had been stripped from the room for forensics to evaluate. The bare room looked small and pathetic without curtains or a bedspread on the tiny bed.

"Did you notice Mr. Metzger having any visitors?" Ernie asked the man.

"I was busy most of the time. And I'm only here days. My night clerk just came in. You could ask him."

Tim Stryker was the night clerk for the Mountain Arms Motel. He shook hands with the sheriff and deputy, then sat back down in the chair in front of the television.

"How long have you worked here, Tim?" Sharyn asked him.

"Just a few months. I'm trying to get back into the idea of college but so far, I'm just not interested."

Ernie sat down beside him. "Give yourself some time, son. What happened to you with Carrie is a lot to handle."

"If you wouldn't have given me a break about that shooting in the sheriff's office, I wouldn't even be here," he observed wisely. "I don't know if I said it, but thanks."

"You're welcome," Sharyn said warmly. "This is a second chance for you, Tim. Don't waste it."

"I'll try not to, Sheriff."

"We're here about Tom Metzger. You must have heard about his death," Sharyn explained. "Can you tell us anything about him?"

Tim shrugged. "He drank a lot of coffee. He was kind of impatient, you know, like when he called down for a clean towel or something."

"Did you see anyone there in the room with him?"

"Once, there was a woman," Tim told Ernie.

"When was that?" Sharyn wondered.

"Probably one day last week. I think it was the night before he went missing."

Ernie glanced at Sharyn. "Could you describe her?"

"Maybe. She was old. Dyed blond hair. Red dress. When I came to the door with the ice he wanted, he yelled at me because it took so long and she was, like, trying to hide behind him."

"Have you ever seen her before?"

"I don't think so."

"Are you sure about the day you saw her here?"

"Pretty sure. The deputy came two days later."

"Why didn't you tell him about the woman?" Sharyn wondered.

He shrugged. "He didn't ask. He just took the stuff out of the room and left. He didn't say much of anything."

Sharyn's lips thinned in annoyance.

"Think you could tell someone how to make a sketch of this woman?" Ernie asked him.

Tim grinned. "Like on televison?"

"Just like that."

"Sure."

Sharyn made arrangements with the motel owner. They would take Tim to the sheriff's office to make the sketch, then bring him back.

"How old do you think the woman was?" Ernie asked her while they waited for Tim to grab his shoes.

"Probably around forty-five, like Metzger," Sharyn replied with a smile.

"That's what I was afraid of," Ernie answered. "What does that make me?"

"Don't ask."

Ernie called ahead for their sketch artist to meet them at the office. They didn't need and couldn't afford to keep one on staff, so they made do with a local artist who helped them out from time to time.

While Tim was tucked away with the artist in a side office, Ernie and Sharyn met with Ed and Joe. They'd come in from canvassing the boaters and fishermen in the lake with nothing more to show than some sunburn. David came in halfway through the discussion. Sharyn asked to see him in her office when they were finished.

There wasn't much to do on the Metzger case until they heard back from forensics about the cup. Sharyn sent Joe out to investigate an argument between two spouses in the county and Ed to settle a dispute between two farmers over a fence.

They waited, having coffee and talking to Trudy, until David had slammed the door coming out of Sharyn's office.

"Took him down a peg or two," Joe said as the other man rushed by.

"He's been kind of out of touch since he started up with Regina," Ed defended. "A woman can do strange things to a man."

"If the sheriff sees you two out here talking about it, there's gonna be another woman doing strange things to two men," Trudy reminded them pointedly.

They laughed, but they left the office behind the other deputy.

"I'm going out to take a look at that convenience store tape that the manager says shows the guys holding up his store," Ernie told Sharyn when he thought it was safe to go into her office.

"What?"

"The tape, oh, never mind. I'm working the robbery at that convenience store."

"All right," she answered, preoccupied. "Be careful."

"You're fair, Sheriff. David had it coming. He wasn't paying attention to his job. He should have asked the Stryker boy the questions he was supposed to ask."

"I know, Ernie," she said flatly. "I'll see you when you get back."

Sharyn decided to head out to Mary Sue Anderson's house while everything else was slow. She saw David taking off in his patrol car as she left the lot and shook her head.

David was the one man in the department she felt she wasn't making headway with since taking over as sheriff. He had been with the department longer than her by two years. They were the same age, graduated from Diamond Springs High School the same year. He was a good deputy. Sometimes she felt that he resented her because she took over from her father. There seemed to be an authority problem. He didn't want her telling him what to do.

But she couldn't let carelessness go by without commenting on it. He was wrapped up with Regina. Everyone knew that. But not to have questioned the motel clerk was inexcusable.

His attitude had been hostile and angry. He hadn't said much. What he had said wasn't any form of apology or attrition. Sharyn hoped he would cool down and see that he was in the wrong. She would hate to have to let him go.

Mary Sue Anderson's house was a cookie-cutter duplicate of the Bost house next door to it. Small windows, tin roof, big porch. It was as though some builder had come through Diamond Springs seventy years before and created row after row of houses exactly the same.

Mary Sue was sitting on her front porch swing, a glass of cold lemonade in her hand. She was wearing a white cotton dress. Her hair was thin but dyed brown. Her face was a series of smile lines, testifying to the fact that she had lived a good life without Captain Bost.

"Mrs. Anderson?" Sharyn asked as she approached the porch.

"Sheriff! Come on up! This is my granddaughter,

Katie. Katie, get the sheriff some lemonade. Hot as it is out today, she needs somethin' cool to drink."

"I got your message about coming by and talking with you."

"You're Selma's niece! She and I play bridge together every Tuesday. She's so proud of you!"

"Thank you, ma'am." Sharyn went up on the porch and sat down on a chair, taking off her hat. "It's a hot one today."

"Yes, it is! I think it's getting hotter, Sheriff. I really do. I don't think it was this hot when I was a child."

Katie came back with a smile and a glass of lemonade, then excused herself to go inside and play with her Nintendo.

"Children today," Mary Sue reminisced. "Always around that box! No time for anything else!"

"Times do change," Sharyn agreed. "I'd like to speak to you about Captain Bost, Mrs. Anderson."

"Call me Mary Sue. Everyone does, Sheriff."

Sharyn smiled and sipped her lemonade. "All right. Mary Sue. You can call me Sharyn. What can you tell me about Billy Bost?"

Mary Sue smiled and for an brief instant, Sharyn could see the face of the lovely young woman she had once been. The blue eyes sparkled and the lined cheeks blushed.

"Billy Bost. He was a hero, you know. The only one from this town to be cited for bravery during the war. And he loved me. That boy worshiped the ground I walked on!"

"How did you feel about him?"

Mary Sue smiled. "He was so handsome! Tall, big arms and shoulders. A full head of curly dark hair. I couldn't believe it the first time he asked me out."

"You stared dating in high school?"

"Well, officially, yes. But we knew we loved each other sooner than that. He was a thoughtful man. Always brought candy for my mama. Always shook my daddy's hand. He never forgot to say please or thank you. And industrious! That man was making money before he was twelve! Mowing lawns, delivering papers, washing windows. He was a good man. A hard-working man."

A wizened old man pushed open the screen door and joined them.

"This is my husband, Delbert Anderson. Del, this is Sheriff Sharyn Howard, Selma's niece."

"Howdy, Sheriff," Del acknowledged her.

"Mr. Anderson." Sharyn shook his hand. "I'm here talking with your wife about Billy Bost."

"Billy? That was a long time ago!"

"Well, you know we found his plane in the lake," Sharyn suggested.

"I heard. I couldn't believe it after all these years!"

Mary Sue shook her head. Her eyes were unfocused, seeing into the past. "He was a hero," she whispered.

Del sat down beside his wife and took her hand. "What can we help you with about Billy, Sheriff?"

"The problem is," Sharyn told them, looking at the old couple, still obviously in love, "it appears that Billy might not have died the way everyone thought."

"What? We all saw him," Del remarked.

"Not you," Mary Sue replied. "Remember? You were at work that day at the factory. I was in the yard with Mama and Daddy. The Bosts were out in their yard too, watching as Billy went by in his bomber. But you were at work, Del."

Del glanced up at Sharyn then glanced down again.

"I guess I was. I've heard it so many times, I feel like I was there."

"Maybe you could tell me what you remember," Sharyn suggested. "Until this week, a lot of younger people thought the whole thing was only a story."

"Well, we were all standing outside, watching Billy's plane. There were people who'd come out of their houses all around town because everyone knew we were watching for him that day. Everybody was so excited!" Mary Sue told her.

"It was like when the circus came to town," Del explained.

"Anyway, here comes Billy in his shiny plane. He was flying so close, I thought I could see him in his leather jacket and goggles but my mama said it was my imagination. He dipped his wing to me. Like he was saying 'I'll see you later, Mary Sue', then there was a loud noise, like a backfire, and the plane went straight down. I couldn't believe it. And that awful sound it made. I'll never forget that sound." She shuddered, her slight frame quivering.

"We should go inside," Del said, looking at her. "It's too hot out here, Mary Sue."

"My heart was broken that day," Mary Sue continued. "I never really recovered. Billy was my one true love. Del has been good to me and we have a fine family. But Billy. Oh, Sheriff, he was just a special man."

Sharyn glanced at Del Anderson. He had looked away. "Did you call Mr. Metzger about the plane, Mary Sue?"

"Yes, I did, Sheriff. I read in the paper that Mr. Tom Metzger was making a movie about another lost pilot in Utah and I wrote him and told him Billy's story about how he went down and that they'd never found his plane or him."

"You called that author fella?" Del asked in surprise.

Mary Sue nodded. "I thought he could find Billy and give him a decent burial."

"So then, Mr. Metzger contacted you about the story?"

"His secretary did, yes. He came here and I showed him my scrapbook. He decided right then that he should write a book about Billy. He said he thought they might make a movie."

Sharyn looked at her excited face. "Do you know of anyone who didn't think Billy was a hero? Who didn't like Billy or would have wanted to kill him?"

"Kill Billy?" She was aghast. "Everyone loved Billy."

"That's the truth, Sheriff," Del confirmed. "Everyone loved Billy."

Mary Sue put her hand to her chest. "Bobby always thought it was Nazi sabotage. Was he right?"

"Mary Sue, I don't want this to get around yet but I think someone shot Billy. While he was flying low over the lake. I think the backfire sound everyone heard was gunfire. When we brought up his plane, his skull had a hole in it. Do you have any idea who could have done that?"

"Nazis," Del spat out. "They were everywhere!"

"It would have been someone with a high-powered rifle and he or she had to be an excellent shot."

Mary Sue lost all the color in her face and almost fell off the swing. Sharyn jumped to her side and supported her in her arms while her husband tried to lift her.

Chapter Six

Between them, they were able to get Mary Sue from the porch to the sofa in the living room. Katie went to call the doctor and Del knelt at her side, begging her to wake up and come back to him.

Sharyn offered to call an ambulance but Del wouldn't hear of it. He wanted their doctor, not some young quack who would just want his wife for an organ donor.

"Mary Sue's not strong," Del told her. "Her heart is giving out."

"I didn't mean to upset her, Mr. Anderson, but if Billy was shot and killed, I'll have to investigate."

"It was over fifty years ago!" Del pointed out.

"There is no statute of limitations on murder, Mr. Anderson. Even a hundred-year-old murder would have to be investigated."

Mary Sue moaned softly.

"The doctor's coming," Katie said as she returned to the room.

"Do you have any thoughts on who could have murdered Billy, besides the Nazis, Mr. Anderson?"

Del shrugged, still holding his wife's hand. "I told those Navy people everything I knew about it."

"Navy people?"

"They came yesterday, Sheriff. Mary Sue was out with Katie and her mother. I didn't tell her because I knew she'd be upset."

Sharyn thanked him. "I hope Mary Sue feels better later."

"Thanks, Sheriff." Del smiled grimly. "It's only a matter of time now. Precious time."

Sharyn walked back out of the house and put her hat on her head. What was going on with the Navy? Those two officers weren't there just to help out with aviation history. What was their connection to Billy's death?

"You had a call from your mother about dinner tonight, Sheriff," Trudy told her as she arrived back at the office.

"Thanks, Trudy."

"And Commissioner Swindoll called to let you know that he'd be monitoring all helicopter activity personally."

"Thanks, Trudy."

"And Nick is waiting in there for you," she warned before Sharyn opened the door to her office.

Sharyn grinned. "Maybe I'll just leave for the day before it gets any worse."

Trudy waved. "Too late for that, Sheriff."

She opened the door to her office and put her hat on the tree near the door.

"Was your grandfather as mean as he looks?" Nick asked as she closed the door.

"Probably," Sharyn replied. "At least as far as the law was concerned. There was no small breach of the law to him. Everything was either legal or not. But he was a good grandfather."

"I guess that's all that matters," he replied, looking down from the picture on her wall to the face of Jacob Howard's granddaughter.

"I know you're not here to ask me questions about my grandfather," she said to him, taking the seat at the front of her desk instead of behind it. "What can I do for you?"

Nick played with the pen he'd found on her desk. "How about dinner? I could break it to you over some manicotti and wine."

Sharyn grimaced. "It must be bad for you to offer food with it."

"You're not gonna like it," he promised. "The tests are back on the remains we found in the plane. Captain Billy Bost was shot and killed by a .45-caliber bullet from a Browning rifle. He would have died almost instantly. The copilot died from injuries sustained in the crash, and since the crash was caused by the shot, his death is a homicide too."

"Great. Someone did murder the hero."

"From the trajectory of the bullet, it looks like someone was standing on one of the hills around the lake. The plane flew in low over the lake, dipped its wings, and *zap!* The shooter had to be a marksman."

"What else?" she wondered.

"I'm afraid it's the same with the coffee cup. There were traces of sleeping pills in it."

"You know, Ernie says his mother crushed all of her medicine in food and drinks to take it."

He nodded. "He doesn't believe Metzger was murdered?"

"The evidence still points more to suicide or accidental death than murder."

"What about the pill bottle?"

"Anyone could have picked that up," she rationalized.

"And people go around wiping their fingerprints clean from everything they touch?"

"I'll give you that. I don't understand why that would have happened. Or how."

"But you don't want to investigate it as a murder?"

Sharyn sighed. "I'm not sure it fits a murder profile. Especially not because of the Bost murder."

Nick stood up and replaced the pen on her desk. "Too bad. I'm filing it as a homicide. That's what it looks like to me."

"You might be getting carried away by the knowledge of the older murders," Sharyn reminded him. "You think someone murdered Metzger because Bost was killed and they were trying to protect themselves. That doesn't have to make sense. The two don't have to be related."

"They don't have to be," he agreed. "But I believe they are and it's up to me to make that judgment on the death certificate. I'm calling it foul play, Sharyn."

She nodded. "I guess you have to call it as you see it, Nick. But I think you might be wrong."

"Are you sure you're not being influenced by this whole thing with the commissioners?"

Sharyn looked at him. "How?"

"You don't want to spend the funds it'll take to investigate three homicides."

"That's not it, Nick! I don't care about that stuff with the commission! But if you're wrong—"

"Then I'm wrong. I'm willing to take that chance to have you investigate it as a murder."

They stared at each other for a long moment over the top of her desk.

"All right," she said, resigning herself to his pronouncement. "If you call it murder, we have to investigate it. That's how it works."

"Thanks."

"Don't thank me. If we can't find anything, or we find it was suicide, you end up looking bad!"

"That's okay."

"We'll get started on it, then." She nodded. "Anything else?"

"That's it," he answered shortly. He walked to the door and paused with his back to her. "What if I was just asking you out to dinner?"

"What?"

He shook his head. "Nothing. I'll see you later."

Sharyn looked thoughtfully at the door after he was gone. Had he asked her out to dinner? Or had he *almost* asked her out to dinner?

Not that it was a big deal either way. She'd had dinner out with Ernie a few times and lunch once with Joe and Ed. They always had a Christmas party at the office. She could go out and eat with Nick. They worked together, after all.

Sharyn had Trudy run copies of everything they had on both cases. She didn't expect anyone back that day but tomorrow they would start out fresh with two homicides on their desks.

She went home, showered, and changed her uniform for a pair of lightweight blue dress pants and a green tunic top. She put on her lipstick and looked at her lengthening hair. It was almost down to her shoulders, longer than it had been in years. John Metzger had said that it looked like it was on fire. That was a good metaphor for it. Maybe she'd get it cut over the weekend.

"Will you set the table, dear?" her mother sang out from the kitchen.

"Sure," Sharyn replied, joining her. She opened the cabinet door.

"No, not that stuff, honey." Faye giggled. "The good china. We're eating in the dining room."

They hadn't eaten in the dining room since her father had died two years before. And her mother giggled.

"What's up, Mother?"

"I wanted to save it as a surprise," her mother told her.

"What?"

"Caison is coming over tonight, Sharyn. He wants us all to get to know one another better."

"Why?"

Her mother slammed the drawer. "Isn't it obvious? We're serious about each other, Sharyn. We might get married."

"Married? You and Caison Talbot?"

"Why is that so hard to believe?"

"Of all the men in this county, Mother, why him?"

"You know we've been friends forever, Sharyn. Kristie likes him. Why don't you?"

"She doesn't know him," Sharyn growled ominously.

"And you do? Outside of that unfortunate incident dealing with that Sommers girl's death, you never speak to him. You never see him. You don't know him. But you could try, Sharyn. For my sake."

Her mother was still pretty when she cried. She did it in a way Sharyn only wished she could emulate. One silent, silver tear slipped down her dainty cheek. Her eyes never turned red and her face never got blotchy. Her lip quivered a little but it added to the overall effect.

"All right, Mom," Sharyn said finally. "I guess I can have dinner with him."

"And be nice?"

"And be very nice," Sharyn amended.

Caison Talbot arrived early. He brought a bottle of good wine. He had a shock of thick white hair and a way of concentrating his blue gaze on people that made him look like pictures of Andrew Jackson. He had been state senator for two terms and had just won a third. He strolled into the house as though he owned it, which made Sharyn clench her hands at her sides. The thought of him sitting in her father's place made her blood boil!

"Good evening, Sharyn," he said to her after he had kissed her mother's cheek. "Interesting case you're working with that author in the lake."

"Good evening," Sharyn responded, looking away from that kiss. "You keep up with everything, don't you?"

"It's my district! Of course I know what's going on. So, you think it was murder?"

"I don't know yet," she answered truthfully.

"That's not what you said to the commission."

"I *know* what I said to the commission."

"Sounds more like suicide or an accident to me, Sharyn. Best watch your step!"

"Thanks," she responded with a glance at her mother. "Is dinner almost ready? Do you need some help in the kitchen?"

"Dinner is almost ready," Faye told them. "I don't need you in the kitchen. Let's go into the dining room and sit down."

Caison opened the bottle of wine and poured himself and Sharyn a glass.

"So they finally found Billy Bost, eh? I was wondering if they would."

"You knew the story was real?" she asked him doubtfully.

"I only knew by hearing it from my parents. I wasn't there personally. But my father knew Billy Bost. Went to school with him. He told me he was a fine man."

"Did he give you any idea about who'd want to kill him?"

"He was killed?" Caison demanded.

Sharyn sipped her wine. "By a high-powered rifle. He didn't lose control and fall into the lake. He was dead before he hit the water." Was she looking smug? she wondered. After all, it was the first thing Caison Talbot *didn't* know.

"Shot?" He shook his head. "Nothing's sacred anymore. Nothing means anything."

"Bobby Bost thinks it was Nazis," she told him.

"He's a fool!"

"How can you be so sure?" she questioned.

He leaned forward as her mother was bringing in

the food. "If he was shot, it was by some jealous deviant who couldn't stand that he was a hero. You can bank on that."

"That's enough of that," Faye censured their conversation. "You know I don't think murder or death are good table talk, Sharyn."

Conversation was lively between the widow and the senator. Sharyn listened as she ate her meal and answered when they spoke to her. Clearly, she wasn't necessary to enhance their time together. She found herself wishing Ernie would call. Or an airplane would fall through the roof.

"When are you up for re-election, Sharyn?" Caison asked her, pinning her with his sharp blue eyes.

"Uh, two years," she replied.

"Good. That might be enough time to forget that whole unfortunate helicopter incident," he told her.

"I didn't do anything wrong," Sharyn said, bristling at his tone.

He pointed his knife at her. "The only thing you did wrong, young woman, is not assigning guilt! If you're going to stay in public office, you're going to have to learn to assign guilt. Let a deputy who doesn't have to be elected take the rap for this. You can slap his hand and go on. You look good. The people are happy."

"I don't have a deputy who did anything wrong," she told him. "And if I tried to do that right now, the commission would probably want me to fire him. They want to make the department smaller. Any excuse would do!"

"I understand." He nodded his head. "But better him than you!"

"Senator!"

Her mother looked at her from across the table, making her eyes well with unshed tears.

"Yes?" he replied.

"Nothing," Sharyn muttered, backing down.

"Coffee?" Faye asked brightly.

Sharyn pleaded a headache and a long day. She went to bed while her mother sat on the front porch with the senator. They were churning ice cream.

She lay in her bed for a long time, staring at the ceiling with her arms behind her head.

Nick was forcing her to investigate Tom Metzger's death. It looked a lot like an accident. Except for the missing, anonymous girlfriend. The department was going to have to investigate Captain Billy Bost's and Joe Walsh's murders. Even if the assailant was seventy years old.

Putting away an elderly person for a murder committed fifty years ago wasn't going to be popular. Even if the murderer was dead and she had to destroy his memory, it wasn't going to be popular.

No one would care much about Tom Metzger, sorry to say. He wasn't from Diamond Springs. The only thing interesting about him would be the fact that he found the plane in the lake.

Could Nick be right and the two incidents be linked?

She could see where Nick would think so. If the person who killed Billy Bost was still alive, it would make sense that they would want to keep the plane from coming up with the evidence. All these years, no one had a doubt about what happened to the hero. Except for his family, and they believed he was killed by the Nazis. The killer was safe.

Suddenly, here comes Tom Metzger, raising the

dead and a lot of questions that would be hard to answer.

Somehow, it was just difficult for her to imagine a seventy-year-old man or woman drugging Tom Metzger's coffee and pushing him in his truck into the lake. She imagined it was going to be difficult for a jury to believe as well.

Of course, it could have been a relative or friend of the septuagenarian. Someone who knew about the murder and was willing to help cover it up.

She closed her eyes, deciding she would put it all in front of her deputies and take the high road. Whatever the general consensus was about the crime, they would have to pursue it. If they looked at everything and couldn't actually find evidence of a crime, she would have to file that as well.

And what was going on with the Navy investigating behind her back without so much as contacting her office? What was their part in all of this? What did they know that they weren't sharing?

She went to sleep thinking about the mystery woman in Tom Metzger's life, wondering what part she played in it all. Until she located her, Sharyn knew there would be a piece of the puzzle missing.

The next morning, they met in the interrogation room, files in hand.

Nick was there with a briefcase full of material. Sharyn nodded to him and closed the door behind her as she entered the room.

"Did someone call David in for this?" Joe asked as they were settling down with coffee and folders.

Sharyn pulled out her chair. "David handed in his resignation this morning, effective as of today. I'm afraid we're facing a triple-homicide investigation with one man short."

"Resigned?" Joe couldn't believe it.

"He said I made him look silly. That he was doing his job and he wasn't being affected by his girlfriend."

Ernie shook his head and fingered his moustache.

"The kid doesn't know his own mind," Ed said quietly.

"If we can get on with this?" Nick brought them back to the table. "I have some other things to do today."

They all took their places, glancing at Nick and Sharyn.

"All right," she began. "Let's start with the Metzger case. Nick is filing his report as a homicide. That means we'll have to investigate."

"A homicide?" Joe demanded. "Looks like a suicide to me!"

"There are a few things that don't fit together," Nick replied darkly. "First of all, where did he take the sleeping pills? He couldn't have taken the pills and made it to the lake. At least not in my estimation. That means he was working at the lake and decided to dose himself with a whole bottle of sleeping pills, then got into his truck and fell asleep at the wheel while the truck went down the ramp."

Ed shrugged and glanced around the table. "Sounds possible. It could have been an accident."

"It may be," Nick agreed grudgingly. "But there's also the question of the bottle. Where is it? If he was too groggy to know better, he would have dropped the bottle. It would have been in the trash or in the truck."

"Unless he had it planned this way," Ernie suggested.

"Even so," Nick argued. "If you had the whole thing planned, where would you put the bottle? There's no packaging. Nothing. Most people committing suicide don't think about what they do with the empty pill bottle."

Joe and Ed shifted their feet and everyone looked at their folders.

"Then, if you'll notice, there are no fingerprints. On anything. Try to find that in your own house. Someone had to wipe the prints clean in the motel and on the truck. Why would Metzger do it? If he'd committed suicide, what would it matter? He would want us to know he did it. If it was an accident, everything would have been as he left it."

"It's true, there is no note," Ernie added halfheartedly.

"Which brings us to murder number two," Nick continued with a glance at Sharyn, who nodded and looked at her file.

"The captain was murdered. He was shot in the skull by a Browning model 1885 BPCR Creedmore rifle. The bullet was still there on closer examination. There was no exit wound. It would have lodged in the brain at the time. He was probably still alive when he hit the water but died shortly after. He wouldn't have been able to control the plane. The copilot probably wasn't able to take over quickly enough. The copilot's death would count as a homicide too."

"So, we have to look for a murderer that's at least seventy years old?" Joe asked, scratching his head. "That'll be popular."

"For the captain's murder," Nick agreed. "For Metzger's, I think it could have been a relative of whoever shot the captain. They knew Metzger was going to raise the plane and wanted to stop him. There was no way for them to know that his brother would come and do the thing anyway."

"So, we're going on the assumption that the two are combined? Maybe even by the same person?" Joe asked.

Everyone looked at Sharyn.

"I think there are some other questions that need to be answered," she began, taking over from Nick. "First of all, who is this mystery woman who may have visited Metzger at his motel before he died? Is she involved in all of this? We need to look until we find her. Tim Stryker told us that there was a woman with Metzger at the motel the night before Metzger died. And we're still checking out both Metzger brothers. It's possible that the two murders are combined but I'd like to play it safe and check out the two murders independently."

Joe snickered. "You? Play it safe, Sheriff?"

She smiled. "This one time. At least until we have answers for some of these questions. I don't like loose ends. Since David's not here, we're going to have to take turns working night shift until we can find a replacement."

"You could call in one of the deputies who are trained for emergencies," Ed suggested.

They all looked at Nick.

"I'll think about it," she promised. "In the meantime, we pull a few doubles. I'll start tonight. Ed, you're tomorrow. Ernie, Wednesday; Joe, Thursday; and we'll start again."

"What about Nick?" Ed asked outright. "He's trained."

"Nick has his hands full with this investigation," she

countered. "This is the schedule for now. Then we repeat. Try to keep track. As far as the two cases are concerned, Ed, you and Joe will work the first murder, Captain Bost. I want all the details you can get together on his life. Yearbooks, any friends still left alive. See if anyone else saw the plane go down. Let's find out if the captain had any enemies. Maybe someone saw something that day and they kept quiet or didn't realize what they saw."

"Investigating a hero this town has made into legend?" Ed smiled. "I thought you said you were going to play it safe."

"I think the man had one enemy, despite everyone's assumption that they all loved him. Someone shot him. I want daily reports. Ernie, you and I will be checking out Tom Metzger and the mystery woman. She's out there somewhere and she might have the answer for us. Also, the colonel's wife."

"What about the Nazi theory?" Ernie asked. "There were reports of Nazis being in this country."

"I don't buy it," Sharyn replied. "Unless we can find some evidence that the Nazis were involved."

They all nodded and started getting to their feet around the table.

"Sheriff," Ed asked before he walked out the door. "Will you hold up filing anything on David's resignation until I have a chance to talk to the boy? I know he doesn't deserve it, but he's a good deputy. I hate to see him go down this way."

She nodded. "I don't want to lose him, either, but he has to see that he can't work the job thinking about Regina to the extent that he forgets everything else. If you think you can get him to see that, I'll hold the position."

"Thanks," he replied. "I promised his mama I'd look after him."

"Do what you can," she agreed.

Ernie shuffled toward the door. "I'll be on the phone with my New York contacts about Metzger. I still haven't been able to reach the colonel's wife. But I'll keep trying."

"All right," she said. She looked up to find herself in the room alone with Nick.

"You could have backed me up," he said quietly.

"I don't know if you're right," she answered truthfully. "If we start putting the two together, we might get the wrong answer and a killer could go free."

"I could do the deputy job," he added, changing the subject.

"I think we'll be okay for now," she said, glancing up at him. "If not, I'll be the first one on the phone to you at three A.M."

"You know," he began, walking closer to her, "you asked me before if I had a personal problem with you on the job."

"I remember."

He looked closely at her. "Well, Sheriff, do you have a personal problem with *me* being on the job?"

She didn't blink. "Not at all."

"Good." He nodded and picked up his briefcase. "I'd hate to think you had personal feelings about me."

She looked at his retreating back as he left the interrogation room. She would have asked him what he meant, but she'd given up long ago trying to understand Nick.

Trudy met her at the door. "The colonel is waiting for you in your office, Sheriff."

Sharyn grimaced. "Thanks."

"Should I forward any calls to your office right away?"

"No, that's okay," Sharyn told her. "I can handle the colonel."

He was standing at the side of her office, looking at the pictures on her wall.

"Your father?" he asked when she walked into the office.

She closed the door behind her. "Yes. And my grandfather."

"Your father must have been disappointed not to have a son to carry on the family legacy," he observed.

She shrugged. "He might have been. I don't think he ever thought about it."

"But you stepped up and took his place when he died?"

"That's about it."

He turned to face her. "And the ungrateful members of this community don't realize what you do for them, do they? Civilians!"

She took her seat behind her desk. "Is there something I can do for you, Colonel?"

"I heard that you're planning on treating my brother's death as a homicide."

There was only one person he could have gotten that information from. David. She didn't believe Ed, Joe, Ernie, or even Nick would have told him.

She nodded. "The medical examiner sees it that way."

He sat in one of the chairs opposite her. "It sounds insane to me. But suicide is out of the question. My brother wasn't the type."

"Even though he was a coward?" she asked.

He frowned. "Tom was a coward and that's why he

wouldn't have committed suicide. He might have hired someone else to pull the trigger, but he couldn't have done it. I have great respect for people who know when they've fulfilled their purpose and can finish the job."

"Do you have any idea who could have wanted your brother dead?" she asked, knowing she had asked before.

"As I told you, Sharyn, my brother wasn't the type to engender those kinds of strong feelings in people. He lived in his own little world. He did what he wanted to do. I can't imagine him being threatening enough that someone would hurt him."

"What about the woman he was seeing? The clerk at the motel told us that a woman was there the night before Tom disappeared. He said she was in her forties, with blond hair, and that she looked like she was hiding behind him."

John Metzger shook his head. "I don't know. If his agent doesn't know, or any of his friends, I would be the last to know. We didn't see each other unless he wanted me to do something for him. Otherwise we stayed out of each other's way."

"What about your wife? Was she close to your brother?"

He raised his eyebrows. "You've been investigating *me*, Sheriff?"

"I've been investigating *everyone,* Colonel."

The artist from the college knocked on Sharyn's door and she called for him to enter.

"Sorry this took so long," he apologized, handing her a piece of paper. "Tim went back and forth so many times, it was hard to get a clear picture of the woman, but I think we finally got her."

Sharyn looked at the picture. It was a black-and-white drawing of a woman's face. She was pretty, but her eyes were worried and her mouth had a tight line of fear about it.

"Thanks, Hubert. I appreciate it."

"No problem, Sheriff. I keep them for my résumé."

When he shut the door, the colonel asked if he could see the drawing. Sharyn handed it to him then sat back in her chair.

"Do you recognize her?"

He didn't speak for a moment, then he looked up at her and smiled. "No. She's a lot older than his usual lady friends. Unless your motel clerk was wrong about her age. Tom usually likes models. Young, beautiful, and eager to please. This isn't his usual filly."

He handed the paper back to Sharyn. "And for the record, my wife isn't close to Tom, either."

"Mind if we talk to her?"

"Not at all." He scribbled down a phone number on a piece of notepaper and pushed it toward her. "She's in and out a lot. But keep trying."

"Thanks," Sharyn said, taking the piece of paper. "I'm going to have this picture put out on the Internet so that we can reach other cities where she might be known," she told him.

"You think she might have killed him?"

"I really don't know what to think, Mr. Metzger. From your description of his life, no one would have killed him, yet our medical examiner thinks someone did."

"What about the cover-up theory?" he asked blatantly.

She grimaced. "The deputy was wrong to tell you

so much about our investigation, Colonel, I'm sure you know that."

"Well, don't blame him," he replied austerely. "He couldn't hold his liquor last night. He had a lot to get off his chest and I was interested."

"We're investigating the murders of the pilots, in the plane you brought up," she responded as she would with the press later that day. "But whether they're linked is yet to be seen."

"But it is logical to assume that whoever put your brave captain down there in the cold water fifty years ago wouldn't want him brought up. Just look at all the nasty questions that are being asked."

"It may be logical," she agreed flatly. "But we aren't going to assume that as yet."

"Is that the official line?" he questioned her.

"It is," she confirmed.

"Was Tom shot?" he asked quickly.

"No. He wasn't."

"But you're not giving away how he died? Even to his next of kin?"

She shook her head. "Not until the investigation has a chance to proceed. You see what one pair of loose lips got me."

"Me?" he queried, his hard eyes on her face.

"Exactly."

"You could do worse," he observed.

"I'm sure I could," she answered, standing and reaching her hand out to him. "As soon as there's any word, I'll be in touch."

He held her hand a little too long but she didn't look away from his face or show any sign of discomfort.

"I'll look forward to it."

Chapter Seven

Sharyn took a deep breath and resisted the impulse to wipe her hand on her pants. He had that effect on her. She *knew* he was trying to intimidate her and it irritated her.

She didn't believe he was serious about his sharp-eyed flirtation. It was more like he was waiting for her to start giggling and agree to date him. She was only one step better than some silly schoolgirl to him. That rankled.

Ernie knocked, then entered her office, glancing back at the colonel leaving the building. "He's a pistol."

"Is that what you'd call him?" she asked, sitting back down.

"In front of a lady," Ernie replied naturally. "I have some interesting news."

"Interesting and informative I hope?"

He shrugged. "Maybe. A photographer friend of

mine works for the NYPD. For fun, he takes pictures of celebrities he sees around town. He has a picture of Tom Metzger eating dinner with a woman whose description fits this woman." He pointed to the sketch on her desk.

"The colonel said that he had no idea who she was."

"But someone might. Or he could be lying."

She nodded. "Just to make sure that the woman at the motel was the same woman he was dating would be a start."

"My friend is sending me a copy of the picture over the Internet in the next few minutes. I guess if it's the same woman, we can assume she's the mystery woman."

"Can your friend check her out for us? If she is the mystery woman, I'd really like to know who she is."

"I can ask," he replied. "You know, I could have stayed in here with you while you talked to him."

"I know," she told him. "But I don't need you to hold my hand, Ernie. I'm the sheriff."

"And as such, you're entitled to a little respect. I don't see respect in his eyes when he looks at you," he told her fiercely.

Sharyn smiled. "Everything is just a game for him, Ernie. He's trying to get me to back down. It probably undermines his male pride for me to be a woman and an authority figure. I don't believe he's seriously flirting with me."

"But you don't know," Ernie said wisely, "and I'm a man. I know what I see when I see him looking at you."

Sharyn stared at him soberly for an instant, then dissolved into laughter. "Oh, Ernie! That would be scary if it wasn't so funny!"

He smiled. "Maybe to you, but there's nothing wrong with the way you look, Sheriff. You're a fine-looking woman and that uniform doesn't take away from that fact."

"Thanks, Ernie," she replied more soberly. "I'll try to keep him at bay."

"Make jokes!" Ernie mourned, shaking his head. "I'm going to check out that photo."

"Okay. I'm going to start going through Metzger's stuff."

Sharyn took out the box of personal belongings that they had put together from both the work site and his motel. The lab had his clothing, checking it for anything useful. The only things they'd found in the truck were papers from the rental company, and those were mostly ruined by the water.

There was a handful of pens and a tie clasp. He'd picked up business cards from around the area. There was a small notebook with diagrams that looked like a crude drawing of the lake and the shoreline. She closed the notebook and opened his day planner. His handwriting left a lot to be desired but there were a few constants. One set of initials kept popping up. J. M. The initials were scattered over different days with no apparent pattern. They were marked the day before his Caribbean vacation, and again before his book-signing tour earlier in the year. They were in the book on the day before they'd established that he left the city, but there was no mention of them after he'd arrived in Diamond Springs.

Suppose, she considered, they were his girlfriend's initials? Suppose he hadn't expected her to be in Dia-. mond Springs? He'd seen her before he left. Her initials were marked again in two weeks on a Saturday. The day he expected to be home again?

Sharyn wrote down the dates and the initials in her own notebook then closed his planner. If those were his girlfriend's initials, he'd been seeing her since the beginning of the year, at least. From what they knew about Metzger, that was a long time.

She opened up the file folder marked "Diamond Mountain Lake" and looked through the papers. The original letter was still there from Mary Sue Anderson. In it, she described how the plane went down, what she could recall from that day. She told him about Billy Bost and his promising future, cut short by his undying love for her.

He wanted the whole town to know how special I was to him and that he was coming back to me, she wrote. *That's why he died.*

She sent him newspaper clippings and some information about Billy Bost. She told him about Billy's hobbies and sent him a report card and a class picture.

I do not believe Billy lost control of his plane that day fifty years ago, Mary Sue wrote to Tom Metzger. *Neither does his family. We believe he died as a result of foul play.*

Sharyn stood up and reread the paragraph again. Mary Sue had already proposed that something other than pilot error had happened to Billy before Metzger had come to Diamond Springs! But she didn't mention Nazi sabotage as the newspapers and interviews suggested. Metzger's papers didn't show that he had gone to talk with Bobby Bost about his brother. Had he talked to Mary Sue?

Trudy rapped on the door. "Lieutenant Wilkes and Captain Parker of the Navy's propaganda division."

"Is that what they said, Trudy?" Sharyn asked in a low voice.

"No. But they had the nerve to tell me that they were ready to straighten out some questions we might have about Billy Bost."

"Imagine!" Sharyn smiled. "Let them in, Trudy."

"Are you having lunch today?" Trudy wondered. "I could bring something back with me."

"That would be great," Sharyn responded. "Thanks."

Lt. Wilkes and Captain Parker walked stiffly into Sharyn's office. Each clasped her hand in an official handshake, then took their seats at the front of her desk. Their uniforms looked crisp and fresh despite the heat outside.

"What can I do for you, Lieutenant, Captain?"

"It's more what we can do for you," Wilkes replied firmly.

"Oh?"

"The Navy does not want you laboring under any idea that Captain Billy Bost and Captain Joe Walsh died from anything other than pilot error in March 1944."

"It doesn't?"

"No, ma'am," Captain Parker interjected. "The Navy conducted a thorough investigation of the men's deaths in 1945 and 1946. There was no evidence to corroborate anything other than pilot error. The other stories were bogus."

Sharyn considered the young man and woman before her.

He was so cleanshaven that his face showed no hint of a beard. His eyes were clear. His hands were cool and strong. His voice was authoritative and pleasant at the same time. Obviously well trained to deal as a liaison between Naval intelligence and the general public.

She was thin and blond, and her pale blue eyes focused tightly on Sharyn's face. She obviously lacked seniority between the two of them. Wilkes tended to dominate the situation, leaving Parker to catch up or butt her way into the conversation. Sharyn felt as though the young woman was trying to impress her with her sincerity and her command of the subject.

"What were those stories, Captain?"

The lieutenant blinked at that. "Well, ma'am, there were stories that the plane had been shot down. That there was a Nazi sympathizer hiding in the bushes that day. The Navy made exhaustive efforts to find the plane and the bodies as well as investigate the family's fears. We didn't have the technology at the time to locate the plane but I can assure you, there were no Nazis hiding in the bushes that day, Sheriff."

"But Captain Bost *was* shot, Lieutenant Wilkes." She pushed a picture of the captain's skull toward him across her desk. "I don't know if it was a Nazi sympathizer or someone just didn't like him. But the plane went down because he'd been shot. *Not* because of pilot error."

The lieutenant glanced at the captain.

No doubt they were both trying to frame their next words carefully enough to fit the situation, Sharyn mused, watching them.

Lt. Wilkes put the picture back down on Sharyn's desk and looked up at her.

"I appreciate your time, Sheriff. In the light of this new evidence, I'll have to get back to you as far as priorities and what the Navy's stance on this is. I assume this has not been released to the media as yet?"

She shrugged and put the pictures away. "The media is more interested in our other current murder, Lieutenant. Pulitzer Prize–winning author Tom Metzger was found dead here a few days ago. Captain Bost's murder is a little geriatric for them. At least right now."

Captain Parker nodded. "Understood. Thank you, Sheriff. We'll be in touch."

Wilkes stood up quickly and took her hand, giving it a perfunctory shake before he turned on his heel and walked out the office door. Captain Parker was left to trail in his wake.

Sharyn shook her head. The Navy still had an interest in Captain Bost! It was impossible to believe that they still knew his name more than fifty years later. Why would they want to be involved in the investigation? What were they worried about besides looking incompetent?

It occurred to her that maybe there *was* a Nazi sympathizer hiding in the bushes that day. Nothing else made any sense. Maybe they were looking in the wrong direction, if the Navy was involved. Their continued stay in the area was suspicious. They were staying closer than such an old case warranted. Were they worried that she might find something they didn't want to see in print?

Ernie was still waiting for his friend to send the photo. He was also checking with Metzger's friends and other authors who had worked with him.

"I'm going to change my mind and get out of the office," Sharyn told him. "Have you eaten?"

"No," he answered. "I'll probably be along once this picture comes through."

"Okay, I'm going to meet Trudy down at the sub shop."

"How can you eat that stuff?" he asked her, making a face.

"It's good for you," she replied. "Veggies. Cheese."

"Food that's been left out for days, touched by people who don't wash their hands." He shuddered.

Sharyn laughed. "I won't bring you one back."

"Thanks. What did the Navy want?"

"I'm not really sure. I think they don't want us to investigate Billy Bost's death as a homicide."

"Really?" he asked in surprise. "I wonder why the Navy would care?"

"I don't know," she admitted. "Unless there was a Nazi sympathizer or they suspect whoever shot the captain was in the Navy."

"Or he was shot by the Navy by accident," Ernie supplied.

"Accident?" She wrinkled her nose. "That seems a little far-fetched."

He shrugged. "So is the Navy being involved with this. I have a few friends in Naval intelligence. I'll see what I can find out."

"Ernie, is there any place you don't have a few friends?"

He grinned. "The IRS?"

"I'm going to lunch." She laughed. "Let me know if anything pans out."

"I will, Sheriff," he answered, looking at the computer screen.

She walked out of the office and into the wall of intense heat that flowed along the sidewalks and crept up the buildings. A haze of it glimmered across the street. The sky was white with it. Carolina blue skies were for other times of the year. In the summer, it was anything but blue. Then it became Carolina haze.

Still, it was good to get out of the air-conditioning, out of the office, and away from the problems that the triple murders represented. The sun was hot but the big oak trees were very green. Roses nodded in their lazy shade along the sidewalks and the wrought-iron gates.

Nick was walking toward the sub shop, his usual tie and jacket forsaken for the heat of the day. As she watched, Col. Metzger approached him. Nick waited with an impatient frown on his dark face while the colonel spoke, then the two of them walked back toward the hospital.

What was that all about? she wondered, watching them until they walked around the corner of the old Dayton building. What could Col. Metzger possibly have to say to Nick?

"Sheriff?" Ernie called from behind her. "I'm glad I caught you! I think I might have something."

Turning back after a last glance toward the hot street, Sharyn followed him back inside the building. "What's up?"

"Take a look at the photo," he said as he handed it to her. "I think it's a match."

Sharyn looked at the picture. It was a little grainy, but the woman sitting across from Tom Metzger looked very much like the sketch Tim had made with the artist.

"Does he know who she is?" she asked hopefully.

"He says no, but he'll check it out with the waiters at the restaurant and some of Metzger's other haunts. This was taken back in May."

"That sounds promising," Sharyn considered thoughtfully. "I found the initials J. M. all over his planner. It could be this lady."

"Or his brother," Ernie responded. "John Metzger?"

"Maybe," she agreed. "But he has John listed in there. And not as often as J. M. I assumed that was his brother."

"I'll pass that on," Ernie nodded. "Maybe it'll help. In the meantime, I found someone who might be able to help us with the Naval aspect on this anyway. He might know something that can help us on the case and we'll understand why the Navy is involved."

Sharyn nodded. "Okay. Who is it?"

"Retired Admiral George Vendicott. He lives north of Diamond Springs, up near Claraville. He was active on the case in 1946 after he came home from the Pacific."

"Think he'll talk to us about it?" Sharyn wondered.

Ernie smiled. "Already asked. He's writing his memoirs. We can be there by one."

They walked to the back of the building to get a car and Sharyn told Ernie about seeing Metzger with Nick.

"Maybe he's trying to persuade Nick not to look at his brother's death like a homicide," Ernie suggested with a shrug after they were in the hot car.

"Good luck!" Sharyn replied, punching on the air conditioning as soon as Ernie started the engine. "He wouldn't budge for me."

Ernie slid her a side glance. "Then *that's* settled."

Sharyn bristled. "What does *that* mean?"

Ernie pulled out of the garage and into the deserted street. "Nothin'."

"Ernie, I know you don't think Nick ever does anything I want him to do! He's always given me a hard time. You know that."

"You're a good sheriff, ma'am. But you don't know squat about men!"

Sharyn glared at him, then changed the subject.

"What do we know about the colonel's alibi for the time of his brother's death?" she asked coolly.

"According to him, he was on the road, coming here. He didn't stop to spend the night. He drove straight through to Diamond Springs from D.C."

"Not unheard of," she remarked. "But he must have stopped to eat or fill up the tank."

Ernie nodded as he negotiated the ramp that led to the highway out of town. "He did. I have statements from a waitress at a truck stop where he ate and an attendant at a gas station at the Virginia state line. They both recall seeing him."

"At around the time his brother was going into the lake?"

"Not exactly. But the timeline would be tight for him to get here."

"Not impossible?" Sharyn wondered.

"No," Ernie agreed. "Not impossible. But we don't have a motive."

Sharyn considered his point. "How about that he just hated his brother getting all the glory while he got the crumbs?"

Ernie frowned, making his thin mustache droop. "I don't think I'd consider that much of a motive if I was on the jury." He glanced at her. "You think he did the deed?"

"I think he's capable. But I agree with you, he's not a man you'd feel sorry for or think of as being in anyone's shadow."

"What about Nick's theory?"

"That whoever killed Billy Bost killed Metzger to keep him from bringing up the plane?" She shrugged. "I just don't know, Ernie."

"It could be viable," he countered. "If I was responsible for putting Billy in that lake, and fifty-odd years later they were going to bring him up, I might think about it."

"But fifty-odd years later, how afraid would you be of getting caught? What are our chances of tracking down the gun, if it still exists? There won't be any fingerprints. Short of a confession, we don't have much of a chance of finding Billy's killer, Nazi sympathizer or not."

"So you think it was the colonel?" Ernie wondered.

Sharyn took a deep breath. "I think most of the signs point to it being an accident. If someone did kill Mr. Metzger, he or she was very clever. I'd feel a lot better if I knew who the woman was at the motel. I think she's the key."

"If this is a crime," Ernie suggested, "it could go either way. A woman could have done this as well as a man."

"I like to keep up with all the possibilities," Sharyn said. "Here's Claraville. Which way do we go?"

Retired Admiral Vendicott lived in a modest red brick house just outside of town. Not that Claraville was much of a town. The few habitable buildings that were leftover from the ten years that the train stopped at the station there were old and in need of paint. The rest of the town was a funeral parlor and a feed store. Around them, like the ghosts of people who had settled the town, were empty, barely standing wood frames that had once been stores and houses.

George Vendicott was a stocky man who didn't look his age. His head was shaved down to a fine white stubble and his brown eyes were keen on their faces as he answered the door.

"Sheriff!" He took her hand in his huge grip. "I've read about you. It's good to meet you."

"Thank you, Admiral," she responded.

"Call me George. I'm not really an admiral anymore, and retired admiral just sounds like too much trouble. I've got some iced tea ready. Come in."

"Deputy Ernie Watkins, sir." Ernie took the man's outstretched hand. "We spoke on the phone."

"Watkins?" George Vendicott asked, shooting Ernie a troubled look. "Cal Watkins's son?"

Ernie blinked. "That's right, sir. You know my father?"

"Come in," George Vendicott invited, not explaining. "Let's get out of the sun so we can talk."

The retired admiral's house was neat and uncluttered. Its green-and-yellow tones were very fifties but the computer on the desk was one of the latest models, complete with a printer.

When they were settled into the shady room on the leather furniture and each of them had a glass of tea Vendicott looked out of the awning-covered window and frowned.

"So you want to know about the Bost affair?"

"I understand that you investigated the crash in 1946," Ernie stated for the man.

"That's right." He nodded. "I took Joe Ferris's place. The Navy doesn't like to have its planes missing."

"But you couldn't find the plane?" Ernie asked.

"Nope. We used what we had at the time, but it

wasn't good enough. Hated to give up when those boys were down there. If it had happened in the ocean, there wouldn't have been that problem."

"But you did some investigation into the crash as well?" Sharyn inquired, sitting forward in her chair.

"Sure did. I plan to include it all in my book. It's been declassified now. I think it'll make good reading."

"What did you find?" Sharyn wondered, wishing she could get him to come to the point.

George Vendicott sipped his tea. He looked uncomfortable, focusing his eyes on things around the room rather than on his guests.

"Can I use this closing part, the plane being found and the investigation into the crash in my book?" he asked quickly.

"Of course," Ernie replied. "Once the investigation is over and we know what happened, it will be common knowledge. Except for your addition. We can keep that to ourselves, right, Sheriff?"

"That's fine," Sharyn added impatiently. "It never has to go out of this room."

The retired admiral nodded. "The Navy knew that Captain Bost was shot. They knew who did it. They've kept it under wraps all this time."

"Why?" Ernie questioned him. "Why was it such a secret?"

"Who do you think started the whole Nazi sympathizer story?" Vendicott sipped his tea. "The government wanted all Americans to be suspicious of everything that happened. It was a campaign that was set up to save the country in case the Nazis invaded. Misinformation, they called it. It served their purpose."

"Why call it pilot error in a formal statement?" Sharyn wondered aloud, confused by his words. "Why not come out and say it was a Nazi plot?"

Vendicott laughed. "They didn't want to *panic* the country, Sheriff! It was sneaky and quiet this way. Seeping in through the gossip, no one ever knowing the truth, only half suspecting. Put everyone on their toes. Made them feel smarter than the government."

Ernie glanced at Sharyn. She shook her head.

"So, who did kill Billy Bost?" Ernie asked outright.

"I don't know," Vendicott confessed, sitting back in his chair. "I assumed it was a local. But there was one man who had his finger on the pulse of the whole area for the government at the time. He could tell you."

"Who is that?" Sharyn asked, setting down her empty glass on the Native-American sand coaster.

"Cal Watkins," George Vendicott replied quietly. He looked at Ernie's surprised face. "Your father."

Chapter Eight

The drive back to Diamond Springs was accomplished in uneasy silence. Except for barely answered replies to Sharyn's questions, Ernie kept his eyes on the road and his thoughts unspoken.

"Ernie?" she tried one last time as they approached the office.

"Sheriff," he replied with a heavy sigh. "I know you mean well, but this isn't something I want to talk about right now."

"Ernie, it has to do with the case. Your father might have the answer."

"Then it'll go with him to his grave."

He let her out in the parking lot and when she thought he would park the car, he drove back out through the gates. She watched the car disappear down the street, confused and frustrated by his attitude.

She knew he had a problem childhood but she didn't understand his reluctance to talk about his father. He wouldn't even acknowledge what Vendicott had told them about him. It was as though he refused to admit that he existed.

Joe met her as she walked into the cool building after the heat in the parking lot. "Nick's here. Ed's on patrol. I'm not sure where Ernie is, but I thought we could put our heads together and see where we are. Frankly, I feel like a chicken with one leg!"

Sharyn smiled. "How's that?"

"I keep running around in circles," Joe answered.

Nick joined them in the interrogation room. He glanced at Joe. "Did I already miss the conference?"

"This is it," Joe informed him plainly. "We can't seem to find Ernie."

"Ernie isn't missing," Sharyn told them. "He's just not here."

"What's up with him?" Nick asked.

Sharyn related the information they'd been able to get from retired admiral Vendicott. "Cal Watkins is the name he gave us. He's Ernie's father."

Joe nodded. "Okay. What did I miss? Why isn't he happy his daddy was working for the government?"

"I don't know the whole story," she responded. "But I know Ernie's father was in prison for a while. He left his family and made their lives miserable. He was an alcoholic. I didn't know he was still alive."

"Start from the beginning," Nick advised. "None of that made any sense."

"It doesn't make sense to me either," she answered shortly. "Ernie wouldn't talk about it when we left the admiral. I have to find him."

"Don't you want to know what the colonel and I were talking about?" Nick asked.

Sharyn nodded. "I noticed the two of you together on the street."

"He asked me to go back over my findings. Offered me money to make it worth my while."

"What did he want you to find? Suicide?"

Nick shook his head. "Accidental death."

"He doesn't inherit," Sharyn told him. "Why would he care?"

"I don't know," Nick confessed. "But I told him to take a hike."

"Bet he liked that!" Joe laughed.

"So, what now?" Nick asked Sharyn.

"We have the photo of the woman with Metzger in New York. It pretty well matches the sketch. We just need a name. I think her initials might be J. M."

"Okay, what do I do now?" Joe asked.

"On the off chance, go by the hotel where Metzger is staying and find out if he's had any female visitors since he's been here. You never know. Maybe the brothers were seeing the same woman. Take the picture."

"Okay, then I'm heading for home," Joe replied. "This double-shift stuff is killing me!"

Sharyn saw Lt. Wilkes and Captain Parker enter the office and stop at Trudy's desk. "Can you stay?" she asked Nick. "This might be interesting."

Trudy showed the officers to the interrogation room, then left in a huff. Sharyn closed the door behind them and took her place at the scarred wooden table.

"You know we talked with Admiral Vendicott, don't you?" she asked, preferring to take them by surprise.

Captain Parker nodded while Wilkes was still taking a seat beside Nick. "We know."

"Although I'm not sure what you gained," Wilkes told her.

"A name," Sharyn replied. "That's all you need sometimes."

"What do you want to find, Sheriff?" Parker asked her bluntly.

"The truth," Sharyn replied.

"And you think you're going to do that by interviewing old men who scarcely know their own names anymore?" Wilkes demanded.

"You must think so," Nick answered. "Or you wouldn't be here."

"What does the Navy want out of this?" Sharyn queried sharply.

"The Navy is only interested in keeping a low profile in all of this," Wilkes replied in a flat tone.

"Was the Navy involved in Captain Bost's death?" Nick asked, looking at the two officers closely.

Captain Parker glared at him. "No! The Navy would never—"

"They'd just use it for their own gain," Sharyn remarked. "By not telling the truth, the Navy was able to use Captain Bost's death for their own purposes. Misinformation, I believe the admiral called it."

"Call it what you like," Wilkes replied, standing. "The Navy will deny any half-truths you set out about the captain's death. Whatever your investigation turns up, we had no prior knowledge of the event."

"Or the people involved?" Sharyn demanded.

"Exactly," Captain Parker added, getting to her feet. "The entire incident was unfortunate but the Navy was not involved."

"What do you think Cal Watkins will have to say

on that subject?" Sharyn wondered as the two officers were leaving the room.

Lt. Wilkes turned back to her with a nasty smile. "I wouldn't count on anything that old man has to say as evidence. I don't think you'd want to put him on the witness stand."

The two officers left Nick and Sharyn in the interrogation room and disappeared back through the office door to the street.

"So, they knew that Captain Bost had been shot and they knew who shot him, but they covered it up to use it as a propaganda ploy?" Nick asked when they were alone in the room. "They wanted people to think the Nazis could have done it."

"I guess so," Sharyn said, taking in a deep breath. "When the war was over, they didn't want anyone to know what they had done. So they just kept quiet."

"Try to prove it!" Nick snorted.

"I don't have to," Sharyn answered firmly. "All I have to do is find out who killed Billy Bost. Cal Watkins might still be able to help with that."

"Need help?" Nick offered.

"Thanks," she said with a smile. "But I have to find Ernie. I want him there when I talk to his father."

"Okay."

"I would like you to do what the colonel asked. Go over everything you can find on Metzger."

He frowned. "What are you looking for?"

"I don't know," she answered truthfully. "But let's make sure we haven't missed anything. There was a woman in his motel room. Can we find any trace of her? Hair, nails, perfume? Check it out for me, Nick. You were the one who wanted this to be a homicide," she reminded him.

"All right!" He groaned. "If I can't find anything else, I'll back off and give you and the colonel both what you want. Accidental death."

"Thanks," she replied, walking him to the door. "I'll let you know what we find out with Ernie's father." She turned back to Trudy. "I need a car," she told Trudy. "And I need Ernie. Where is he?"

"He hasn't checked in, Sheriff," Trudy told her. "I can buzz Joe or Ed."

"Buzz Ernie," she told Trudy. "He's somewhere around here."

Trudy made the call and handed the phone to Sharyn. "I got him."

Sharyn picked up the phone. "Ernie?"

"Sheriff."

"I need you, Ernie. We need to talk. And I need to know where to find your father."

There was silence at the end of the line. Sharyn thought he might hang up on her.

"I'll be there in five minutes, Sheriff. Pick you up in front."

"Thanks, Ernie."

Ernie was already at the curb when Sharyn walked down the stairs. She swung into the car beside him and he started driving down Main Street.

"Do you want to go somewhere and talk?" she asked him, looking at his taut profile.

"No, I'm fine, Sheriff. And it's a long drive out to the home where my father lives."

"He lives at a nursing home?"

"He hasn't aged well. He's got premature senility according to the doctor. Some days he's good. Some days he's bad."

"Ernie, I didn't realize he was still alive."

He shrugged but didn't look at her. "I don't see him often and I talk about him less."

"I know."

There was a heavy silence between them that Sharyn struggled to find a way to break without making things worse.

"The admiral could have been mistaken. Your father might not have been involved. This could be part of the whole Navy cover-up."

Ernie shook his head, his mouth a thin line beneath his graying mustache. "It wouldn't surprise me if he was directly involved."

"Do you think he might remember?"

"Maybe. If it's a good day. If not, he won't know anything," he explained to her. He glanced at her. "What are you going to tell everyone else?"

She shrugged. "I don't know yet. I guess we'll see if your father remembers anything."

"I'm sorry I walked out on you, Sheriff," he apologized.

"I understand. You know, I've had some questions about my father's conduct."

"But your father wasn't in prison and he didn't beat your mom and you," Ernie added. "You wouldn't even dream of accusing him of murder."

"You're right," she admitted slowly, realizing the pain that he was in. "I don't know what to say, Ernie. But we have to follow this lead."

"I know. And I want to follow it. I guess I just hoped everything was as bad as it would ever get with him. But I want to know if he was involved."

"We could keep his name out of the investigation, as far as the press is concerned," she offered.

Ernie smiled at her. "Thanks, Sheriff. It might not

matter anyway. He's gotten worse in the last year. Last time I was here, he didn't know me."

The nursing home was well kept. Several white brick buildings dotted a graceful landscape of green grass and benches, picnic tables and trees. The lobby was clean and well organized. Ernie told the smiling woman at the desk his father's name and she directed him to the sunroom at the back of the building.

Ernie favored his father. They were both short and wiry. They both had the same hooked nose. The elder Watkins was thin to the point of bare bones. Unlike Ernie, he had a head full of white hair. He looked up at Ernie from his wheelchair.

"Well, you took your time getting here!"

"Sorry, Dad."

"You know I can't wait around like this. Where have you been?"

Ernie glanced at Sharyn then sat down in a chair near his father. Sharyn sat beside him, glad to let him do the questioning if he could get through to his father.

"Dad, do you know anything about Billy Bost getting shot?"

Cal nodded and stared out the window. "I know as much as I want to know about it."

"What's that, Dad?" Ernie questioned.

"I know what's important."

"What's important, Dad?"

"Billy Bost was murdered. As sure as I'm sitting here today. He was murdered before that plane went into the lake."

Sharyn and Ernie exchanged looks. Ernie nodded grimly.

"What happened to him, Dad?"

Cal nodded and focused his eyes on the past. "I

heard that sound. That wasn't no backfire from the plane. It was a shot."

"Did you see who fired the shot?"

"I ran through the trees and I saw him putting the gun away. The plane already hit the lake and everyone was trying to get out to it. Trying to rescue those men."

Ernie frowned. "Did you fire the shot, Dad?" He held his breath.

Cal fixed him with clear brown eyes that mocked him as they always had. "Don't be a fool!"

His son was visibly relieved not to have to add murder to his father's list of sins. "Who fired the shot then, Dad?"

"The G-men want it covered up."

"You can tell me now," Ernie persuaded. "I work for the G-men."

"What's in it for me?" Cal growled with a sharp look at his son.

Ernie shrugged, obviously embarrassed by his father's talk. "I could see about getting you more television time. You'd like that."

"I would," Cal agreed with his son. "They turn the thing off before the good part. All right. We'll play a little guessing game."

"Dad!"

His father chuckled. "There was a man who was courting Mary Sue right under Billy's nose. Billy was so busy being a hero, he didn't notice. Mary Sue didn't realize."

"Who was it?"

"He wanted her for his own. But he kept it real quiet. There was only one way. He had to make sure

Billy's luck didn't bring him back home again. It was his last chance."

"Who, Dad?" Ernie demanded impatiently.

His father turned his head to look at him. "Who else? Del Anderson."

"Are you sure, Dad? It was Del Anderson you saw with the gun that day on the hill?"

"You know I like those cookies with the raisins best," his father told him. "Where's my coffee, Sheryl? You know I like my coffee first thing in the morning. On the table! Don't make me raise my voice!"

Ernie tried again to get his father back to reality but it was no use. Cal was lost in the past, but he wouldn't talk about Billy Bost's murder.

"Sorry, Sheriff," Ernie apologized. "I guess we were lucky to get that out of him."

"Del Anderson?" Sharyn mused as they left the nursing home. "If what your father is saying is true, it would make sense."

"That he was willing to kill Billy Bost to keep Mary Sue?"

"Why not?" she wondered. "People have killed each other over less."

"My dad's testimony would never stand up in court," he reminded her.

"I know," she agreed bleakly. "Del will have to confess."

"If he thinks we have it all, maybe he won't feel bad filling in the details," Ernie suggested.

Sharyn nodded. "Let's take a swing by their house and see how Mary Sue is doing."

She thought back to that day when she was talking to Mary Sue. Had she known and was too afraid to admit it? Was that why she had written to Tom Metzger in the first place? It could account for her violent reaction to Sharyn's suggestion that a marksman had shot and killed Billy before he went into the lake.

"You didn't know your father worked for the government during the war, did you?" Sharyn asked him.

"If he ever did anything on the right side of the law, I didn't know about it," Ernie replied dryly. "They must have picked him for this because he wasn't particularly honest and didn't mind keeping a secret."

"The admiral sounded like he did a lot for the war effort," she reminded him.

Ernie shook his head. "The admiral also was willing to keep a murder secret to further the government's propaganda effort."

"Is he why you decided to go into law enforcement?" Sharyn wondered.

"No," he responded slowly, glancing at her. "A good friend of mine whose father was the sheriff got me into it. Your granddaddy was more like a father to me than my father ever was. Your daddy and I were like brothers."

Sharyn smiled at him. "And now you're keeping his daughter straight?"

"More like watching her back," he answered with a laugh as he turned into the Andersons' driveway. "This isn't going to be a popular arrest, if we have to make one." He shook his head. "What jury is going to send a seventy-year-old man to jail?"

"If he murdered Billy Bost, we still have the obligation to see him make reparation for it, even if it's not anything more than a trial and an admission of guilt."

Ernie smiled and looked at her quickly. "You

sounded just like your daddy just then. He would have done the same thing."

"Thanks." She smiled in return, then looked up at the big white house. "Well, here goes."

They walked up together and knocked on the door. Katie, the Andersons' granddaughter, let them in. Del was out getting food. Mary Sue was resting. Would they like to wait?

"We'll wait, thanks," Sharyn told the girl who offered them some iced tea.

When she was gone, Sharyn roamed the room curiously. There were memos of a life well spent. Clubs and churches. Del was an associate pastor at their church. Mary Sue sang in the choir. Del had retired from the tire manufacturing plant after thirty years. Mary Sue had won ribbons at the county fair for her biscuits and jams.

"What do you say to people like this, Ernie? How do you suggest that Del murdered a man over fifty years ago?"

Ernie shook his head. "I don't know, Sheriff. I guess it's no different than any other person who might be responsible for a crime. Except that he's older."

"And he's done nothing wrong in fifty years. He's been a good father and a husband. He's been an asset to the community." She paused beside a cabinet made of wood and glass. "Look at this, Ernie."

Ernie joined her at the cabinet. It was filled with trophies and citations. Delbert Anderson had been a skilled marksman. One trophy had a picture beside it of three young people. Billy, Del, and Mary Sue.

"He fits the profile," Sharyn said flatly. "The last ribbon here was from three years ago."

"Do you think Mary Sue knew?" he asked her quietly.

Sharyn nodded. "I think she had her suspicions."

"What about Metzger? Could Del have killed him, too?"

"Sheriff? Ernie Watkins! What brings you back out here?" Mary Sue asked as she came into the room.

Katie brought in three glasses of iced tea and passed them out. She helped Mary Sue settle into a chair near the window then left them alone.

"She's a good girl, like her mama," Mary Sue told them cheerfully.

"I remember Annie. How's she doin?" Ernie asked, sipping his tea.

"She's goin' to school. Doing somethin' with computers. Says it pays good. What about you, Ernie? How's your mama?"

Ernie looked down at his glass. "She died two years ago, Miz Anderson."

"Oh, Ernie, I'm so sorry. I probably forgot. My brain isn't what it used to be."

He smiled sadly. "It's okay. I miss her but she's gone to a better place."

"I know she has. That woman was a saint."

"Thank you, ma'am."

"So, I know you didn't come out here to talk about our families, as nice as that might be. Why are you here?"

Sharyn leaned forward, her glass of tea in one hand, while the ceiling fan whirred above them.

"What was your husband doing last Sunday night, Mrs. Anderson?" she asked the woman.

"Last Sunday night?" Mary Sue frowned. "I'm not

sure, Sheriff. He should be home soon and you could ask him."

"Was he out, Miz Anderson?" Ernie asked helpfully.

"Oh, sure! He was out. He's always out on Sunday night. He plays horseshoes with some men down at the park. He always comes home after I'm asleep."

"So you didn't see him when he came in that night?" Sharyn asked.

"No, I didn't. What's this all about, Sheriff?"

Del poked his head through the doorway from the kitchen. "Katie told me you two were here. Let me get cleaned up and we can have some supper."

"I need to talk to you, Mr. Anderson," Sharyn told him calmly. "I'd rather do it alone."

Del walked into the room and sat beside his wife. The couple looked at them from the recesses of their recliners. "Whatever you have to say to me, Sheriff, you can say to Mary Sue. We don't have any secrets."

Sharyn hated what she had to say and do but there was an injustice to right. There was the matter of the copilot as well, who was indirectly killed as a result of the shot that killed Billy Bost. Both men had lay in a cold, wet grave for over fifty years. They deserved some compassion and their families deserved some closure.

"How well did you know Billy Bost?" Sharyn tiptoed into the coming storm.

"We were friends," Del told her. "It was a long time ago."

"Where were you the day Billy was killed, Mr. Anderson?" Ernie asked.

"I'm not sure. It was a long time ago." He looked at the sheriff and the deputy uncertainly.

"I remember," Mary Sue chimed in. "You were at work that day, Del, remember? You were going to come by and watch Billy's plane fly overhead but you were working."

"What difference does it make?" Del asked slowly.

"We don't think you were at work that day, Mr. Anderson," Sharyn told him sadly. "We think you were out on the shore of Palmer Lake. On the hill by the pine trees. You waited for Billy to fly his plane down close enough to get a clear shot at him."

"That's ridiculous!" Del looked at Mary Sue.

"Is it? You were skilled enough to hit him from that distance, weren't you?"

"Even if I was—"

"And you didn't want him to come back and take Mary Sue away, did you?"

"Where did you get such an idea?" he wondered.

"Del!" Mary Sue demanded pathetically. "Is it true?"

"Of course not, Mary Sue," her husband assured her. "How can you ask that?"

"My daddy told me he saw you putting away your rifle, Mr. Anderson," Ernie told him. "He said you shot Billy Bost then stood there and watched while his plane went into the lake."

The old man hung his head.

"Del?" Mary Sue whispered, holding out her hand.

"He wasn't fit to clean your shoes, Mary Sue," her husband whispered. "He would've come back with that pretty smile and taken you away. So, when I heard he was coming, I took a look around. I found the perfect place on that hill where nobody could see me but I would be close to the plane. I took out my Browning and I shot him. Then I put the gun in the lake."

"But you didn't . . . you wouldn't have." She stumbled over the words needed to accuse her husband of murder.

"If that Metzger fella wouldn't have come up here from the city and started poking his nose around, no one would have known the difference. It was part of the legend. The plane sputtered and crashed into the lake. Pilot error. A blot on Billy's perfect record."

Mary Sue was weeping quietly. Katie had heard her grandmother crying and came running from the kitchen.

"I called Mom, and Dad," she told her grandparents with a worried look at the sheriff. "They said they'll be here right away."

"I *knew*," Mary Sue whispered. "Somehow, I always knew but I was too afraid to say anything. I was too afraid to think it. Then when I saw that woman on television, I wrote Mr. Metzger a letter and he called me about Billy. I knew we were going to find out the truth. I just prayed you didn't kill him, Del. I prayed every night."

Delbert Anderson shuddered and looked away from his wife. "What now? Do you take me in to jail, Sheriff?"

Sharyn nodded. "I'm afraid so, Mr. Anderson."

"No one else knows," he told her quietly. "But I'm not a well man."

Ernie stood up. "What happens to you will have to be up to a jury, Mr. Anderson. Maybe you'd like to get a few things together."

"You can't just take my grandfather away!" Katie yelled at them. "He hasn't done anything wrong! You're just scaring my grandma!"

"Katie," Sharyn tried to explain. "I'm afraid it has to be this way."

"I'm calling the police," the girl told them plaintively.

Ernie put his hand on the girl's shoulder. "Honey, we are the police. Now, help your granddad get a few things together—toothbrush, underwear, a change of clothes. Put them in a bag. We'll wait."

"Come on, Katie," Del said in a tired voice.

Katie looked bewildered but she turned away to help her grandfather into the bedroom.

Sharyn tried to comfort Mary Sue but the woman was inconsolable.

"All these years, I've been with the man who killed Billy. All these years. I ate from his table. We had two children together. I care for him but never like I cared for Billy. I loved Billy. He was the only one for me. When I knew he was never coming back, I let Del talk me into marrying him. What am I going to do?"

By the time Del had packed small bag, his daughter Annie was home. She tore through the house like a cyclone, pushing herself between Sharyn and her mother.

"Just what is wrong with you, Sheriff? The last time you came, Mom was sick all day. Now here you are again, upsetting her."

She looked up and saw her daughter holding her father's free hand, a gym bag in the other. "Just what is going on?"

"We're here to arrest your father, Annie," Ernie told her gently but firmly. "He was responsible for killing another man."

"Killing someone?" She looked at the sheriff. "What is he talking about?"

"Your father killed Captain William Bost and his copilot, Captain Joseph Walsh."

"Captain Billy?" she asked in disbelief.

"I'm afraid so, honey," Ernie replied.

Annie shook her head. "You're not serious! My father never hurt anyone in his life. He wouldn't have killed anyone. He didn't kill a hero!"

Del shook his head at his daughter. "Billy Bost wasn't a hero, Annie. He was a man who didn't know how to look after his own and liked the sound of his own voice. I did what I did because I loved your mother. She deserved better than him."

"What? Dad, you don't know what you're saying. Don't say anything else until I get you a lawyer. You can't take him until I find a lawyer."

"I'm sorry, ma'am," Sharyn said to the other woman. "He's going to have to come with us. If he was my father, I'd find him an attorney as quickly as possible."

"Dad?" Annie looked from her tearful mother to her tightlipped father.

"Best do what she says, Annie. Take care of your mama."

They didn't handcuff him. It was a mutual decision made without saying a word. The man had made a mistake and he would pay for it but he was frail and he wasn't a flight risk. How far could he get?

"We're taking him down to the station for booking and processing. It takes a while so you have time to call someone," Sharyn told Annie and her crying mother and daughter. "We'll be careful with him."

Annie nodded mutely, her eyes welling with tears. The three women huddled together and watched from the window as Del was helped into the back of the patrol car and Sharyn and Ernie left with him.

Chapter Nine

Bobby Bost met them at the office two hours later. A handful of reporters crowded around him as he waited on the steps in the rapidly gathering twilight.

"Is it true?" he asked in total disbelief. "Is it true that Del confessed to killing Billy?"

Before she could respond, a reporter from the *Gazette* asked, "Do you have a statement to make, Sheriff Howard?"

Sharyn nodded. "I'll make a short statement."

They poised with their cameras and pens and eager faces.

"We've arrested Delbert Anderson on the charge of murder in the death of Captain William Bost. We don't know yet what charges will be pending in the death of his copilot, Captain Joseph Walsh."

"This isn't the Tom Metzger murder," the reporter from the *Gazette* observed.

"No, it's not. This murder took place fifty years ago.

We only learned about it when the plane was raised from Diamond Mountain Lake."

"What about the Metzger murder, Sheriff?" another reporter asked her.

"We're still working on that one."

"Let's hope it doesn't take as long as this one," someone quipped.

"What about the report in the *Washington Post* today that named Diamond Springs as part of a Naval intelligence cover-up, Sheriff? Any comment?"

"Not at this time," she replied briskly.

"Is Delbert Anderson responsible for Tom Metzger's death?" the *Gazette* writer asked. "Or am I the only person who knows that two plus two makes four?"

Sharyn looked at him steadily. Word traveled fast. Especially since David and Colonel Metzger seemed incapable of keeping their mouths shut.

"I can't comment on that right now either. That's about it."

She turned away from the crowd.

"Sheriff." Bobby Bost followed her up the stairs. "Did Del kill my brother?"

She nodded. "I'm afraid so, Bobby. He's confessed to the murder."

Bobby shook his head. "They were friends. Del was looking out for Mary Sue while Billy was gone. Why would he have killed Billy?"

"Del was doing more than looking out for Mary Sue, Bobby. He was in love with her. He killed Billy so that he wouldn't come back for her."

"I don't believe it! We've lived next door to him since he married Mary Sue. He couldn't have killed

Billy and sat in church every Sunday and looked me in the eye every day!"

Sharyn shook her head. "I can't explain it, Bobby. I only know what he said."

"I'm thankful my mom and dad are dead and don't have to hear this," he told her. "I just wish I didn't have to hear it."

"Did the Navy know about this? How could they leave us guessing for so long?" he replied angrily.

"It was a long time ago," Sharyn tried to explain. "Things were different. People were afraid. Even the Navy."

Sharyn left him on the stairs and encountered Ernie in the lobby.

"I sent him down for fingerprinting and processing. He seems about as good as he could be," Ernie answered. "This is gonna be hard on the whole community. How many people knew him and thought he was a good guy?"

"What did you make of Mary Sue's answer about where he was the night Metzger was killed?" she asked him as they walked into the office together.

Ernie ran his hand through his thinning hair. "I don't know, Sheriff. He seemed to have opportunity, and if Nick and everyone else is right, he had motive. He just wanted to stop Metzger from taking that plane out of the water. It makes a sort of terrible logic."

"But he's not a coldblooded killer, Ernie." Sharyn argued the side of the angels. "He wouldn't have thought to wipe off fingerprints and get rid of the pill bottle. He wouldn't have used pills at all. He would have shot him like he did Billy."

"But he had everything to lose by Metzger raising that plane, Sheriff," he pointed out to her. "And he couldn't have known the brother would do it anyway. If he could have kept that plane at the bottom of the lake for another fifty years, he would have been safe. Murdering Billy seems to be contrary to his nature too. A man will do strange things to survive."

Sharyn took off her hat and laid it on her desk. "I just don't buy it, Ernie. Unless we get a confession from him, I don't believe it. Check with Mary Sue or Annie. Get the names of those men he was with that night."

"I don't *want* to believe it," he said. "I'll check it out."

Assistant District Attorney Michaelson arrived a short time later. He knocked on Sharyn's office door and nodded to her. "Good job, Sheriff. Although the D.A. wishes you would have made it clearer that you were picking up Anderson for both murders. Particularly for the Metzger murder. That's the big one the press is looking for."

"He's in processing," Sharyn told him briefly, barely looking up from the paperwork on her desk. "And I really don't care what the press is looking for, Michaelson."

"What are our chances of going ahead and getting him for the second murder right away, Sheriff?" he continued, despite her frosty reception.

"Zero to none unless he confesses. We're checking on his alibi right now."

"Are you investigating the connection?" he demanded, getting agitated by her dismissal of him.

"What connection?"

Michaelson looked at her as though she were an imbecile. "The link between Anderson and Metzger. He wanted Metzger dead so that he couldn't raise the plane. Where have you been? Oh, yeah, that's right. You were abducted by aliens!"

Sharyn looked up at him then. "That's not my theory."

Michaelson came into her office and closed the door. He sat down on one of the wooden chairs that fronted her desk. "What is your theory, Sheriff?"

She put her paperwork aside and locked gazes with the man. "I don't have one, Mr. Michaelson. I just don't believe Delbert Anderson killed Tom Metzger."

Michaelson shook his head. "And here I thought you loved a good conspiracy theory! Maybe that's not it, huh, Sheriff? Maybe you just like to buck whatever the most sensible answer is."

"You mean the popular answer, Mr. Michaelson? If so, you're right. I'm interested in the truth, not winning popularity contests."

He stood up, his lips thinning to almost nonexistence. "I want to know when he comes back up. I plan to work out a plea on this rather than take it to court. Our stance is that this man has been a pillar of the community. He's seventy-something years old. This is prime reelection material, if we use it right. For both of us, Sheriff, if you want to get on the wagon."

She smiled at him and stood up behind her desk. "I've never been good at being popular, Mr. Michaelson. If my investigation proves that Del Anderson murdered Tom Metzger, I'll be happy to arrest him for the murder. If not, I can't look the other way because it's more convenient for either of us."

"You know, you're like the Lone Ranger," he charged. "You need to learn to be a team player, Sheriff."

"I am when I'm on the right team," she replied lightly. "I'll let you know when Mr. Anderson is back from processing."

"Good." He sniffed. "Does he have a lawyer?"

"I'm sure he will have before he talks to you," she replied quietly.

He made a face. "We're on the same side here, Sheriff, in case you didn't notice. We do different parts of the same job. But we're both the good guys."

"I know," she acknowledged. "I watch television too."

He left her office without another word. Sharyn asked Trudy to find Ernie. There was another part to this puzzle and she felt it didn't rest in Del Anderson's gnarled hands.

Del looked old and tired by the time they'd processed him and found him a cell in the county jail for the night. He sat across from Sharyn, Ernie, and A. D. A. Michaelson in the interrogation room. His eyes were distant, as though he wasn't truly there with them anymore.

"I can offer you a plea agreement," A. D. A. Michaelson said, taking his paperwork out of his briefcase. It was obvious that he was eager to close both cases and have another feather in his cap. Sharyn's words meant little or nothing to him. "But you'll have to admit to both murders."

"Both murders?" Del asked in surprise.

His lawyer and his daughter knocked on the door and entered the room at the same time.

"He hasn't said anything, has he, Ernie?" Annie asked her old friend.

"No, we only just sat down," Ernie replied, getting to his feet to hold the chair for the lady.

"But he has given a statement," Michaelson reminded them all. "He has admitted to the shooting of William Bost."

"I need a few moments alone with my client," his lawyer said. "Jeff Richards." He shook hands with the other lawyer as he introduced himself.

"Michaelson. Take as long as you need, counselor. Your client isn't going anywhere."

They got up to leave the room. Annie called Ernie back.

"I'd like you to stay," she told him. Her pretty brown eyes were desperate and still damp with unshed tears. "You deal with this everyday. You could help us."

"I can't help you with this," Ernie told her. "I'm a deputy. I shouldn't know what your father tells his lawyer. It would cause problems for me, Annie."

She nodded. "I understand. Thanks, anyway."

He left them alone and closed the door behind him.

"What happened?" Sharyn asked him when Michaelson had gone to take a phone call.

He shrugged. "She wanted my help. She doesn't understand."

Sharyn sighed. "I'm sure she never thought she'd have to."

"Michaelson is going for blood on this," Ernie observed. "He wants him for both murders!"

"He thinks it makes sense," Sharyn explained. "Just like you were saying earlier."

"Everybody's gonna think that, Sheriff. Del doesn't have a chance. I sent Ed out to talk to Mary Sue but it doesn't look good."

"What about your friend? Does he have anything for us yet on the mystery woman?"

"People saw her. But no one recognizes her," he said. "I don't know how we'll ever find out who she is. Metzger kept his mouth shut tight on this. He didn't mind talking about anything else. I've read lots of interviews with him. This woman was different. Special somehow. He didn't want her exposed to all that stuff."

"We do know that she was the mystery woman he was seeing and we know that she was here the night before he died."

"But we can't place her killing him and rolling the truck into the lake," Ernie added. "We're still a long way from proving that Del *didn't* kill Metzger."

"I'd believe she did it before I'd believe Del did it," Sharyn told him as Del's lawyer called them back into the interrogation room. "Let's go."

"We're ready, Mr. Michaelson," Jeff Richards told them as they all sat back down. "We're going to request that Mrs. Tucker stays in the room during this time. Because of his age and his frailty, Mr. Anderson would like his daughter to be present."

"Well, I don't see any need to interrogate the suspect," Michaelson graciously allowed the defense attorney. "He's already confessed. Sheriff?"

"We don't have a problem with that," Sharyn replied as Trudy joined them to take notes.

"Before we begin," Jeff Richards said, "we'd like to say that, because of my client's health and age, he would be willing to forego an expensive and time-consuming trial and plead guilty to the charges. If the D.A. would be willing to cut him some slack on sentence recommendation."

Michaelson nodded. "I certainly don't want to drag your client before a jury for the same reasons, Mr.

Richards. And we are certainly sensitive to the situation. But there is one sticking point I will have to insist on before we enter into any plea agreement."

"That is?"

"He pleads to the Metzger murder as well. Anyone would be able to understand what he went through knowing that his life would be over if that plane was raised. No jury in the world wouldn't be sympathetic to his emotional state. As you said, he is ill and his mental state could be called on to explain what happened."

"A moment," Mr. Richards said as he bent his head to confer with Del and his daughter.

Sharyn glanced at Ernie uncomfortably. There wasn't much she could do if Del agreed to take the blame for the Metzger murder.

"What are you offering in exchange for that consideration, Mr. Michaelson?" Richards asked while Del and his daughter looked on with frightened eyes.

"I'm willing to offer murder two on the first count and manslaughter on the second with a sentence of fifteen years that your client will serve concurrently."

Ernie shook his head. Annie gasped. Del looked down at his hands and closed his eyes.

Richards nodded. "That's a generous offer, Counselor. But while my client is willing to admit to the Bost shooting, he isn't ready to admit to the Metzger killing. He'd rather take his chances with a sympathetic jury."

Michaelson folded his arms across his chest. "I'm afraid I'll have to prosecute for murder one on the Bost shooting as well as manslaughter on the copilot, Joseph Walsh. The best he could hope for is twenty-five to life."

Jeff Richards smiled. "You and I both know that my client would be lucky to survive even a few years of jail time because of his advanced age. What would you be willing to do about first parole?"

"I'd be willing to recommend parole after seven years on the first offer," Michaelson told him. "The other would be fifteen as minimum for parole."

Joe knocked on the door. "They're ready next door for the arraignment hearing."

The A.D.A. nodded. "Think about it, Mr. Anderson, Counselor. That's incredible leniency for murder, even with your client's advanced age."

"What about bond?" Richards asked.

"I don't see any reason to be unreasonable. I don't believe your client poses a threat to the community. We certainly don't see him as a flight risk."

"Thank you," Annie said in a shaky voice full of tears.

The two attorneys walked together while Annie helped her father from the room. Ernie jumped up and offered her a hand.

"What do you think?" Joe asked when Sharyn walked out of the room. "Will Del agree that he murdered Metzger?"

Sharyn shook her head. "I don't know. He's got to be scared. Seven years must seem like a lifetime to him. Imagine fifteen."

"Do you think he did it?"

"I know the theory works for everyone else," Sharyn disputed. "But it just doesn't sit well with me."

John Metzger came into the office with Caison Talbot on one side and Ty Swindoll on the other. Behind them, Sharyn could see a bevy of reporters, waiting for some word about the case, as well as statements from the senator.

"Sheriff." Ty Swindoll was the first to take her hand. "You've done an excellent job."

Caison nodded. "You've made us all proud, what with this Navy investigation and all."

"Even the Navy makes mistakes, sir," Sharyn told him.

"Colonel Metzger would like permission to take his brother's body back to New York for burial, as his brother stipulated in his will," the commissioner told her.

"I feel it's time," Colonel Metzger added, his fierce eyes belying his grief over his brother's death.

Sharyn played for time. She didn't know what good it would do. The possibility was that Del Anderson would agree that he killed both men to avoid a more serious penalty. Everyone else felt that it was likely Del did kill Tom Metzger. Why was she uncomfortable with it?

"I'll sign the papers today. The medical examiner should release him tomorrow, if you'd like to make your plans," she apprised the colonel.

"Thank you, Sheriff. This whole experience has been unpleasant, but you've been very cooperative."

"If you'd step outside with us, Sheriff, we could issue a joint statement," Caison said with a friendly grin.

Sharyn agreed, although the three men who accompanied her to the steps were less than her favorite people.

Caison took his turn stepping up for photos and saying a few words about fighting crime in the small towns in North Carolina, particularly his jurisdiction.

Ty Swindoll said a few words about Diamond Springs and how the citizens worked together with the sheriff's department to solve their problems. Col. Metzger thanked everyone for their help in solving his brother's death. Sharyn smiled and stood with each of them, lending her face for the pictures but not adding any statements.

Sharyn shook hands with all three men. Then she retreated into her office. Nick was waiting there for her, sitting behind her desk.

"You got him!" he congratulated her.

She frowned. "It's a hard thing to feel good about. The man doesn't have so much as a parking ticket in the past fifty years. This is going to ruin his family's life. One stupid act and it's over."

"Fifty years ago, they would have lynched him," Nick reminded her.

"You're right."

"He's had a life to live while Bost has been at the bottom of the lake."

"I know."

"What about Metzger?" he wondered.

She drew in a deep breath. "He didn't say he didn't do it. He didn't say he did. Michaelson is offering a deal he can't refuse."

"But you're not happy about it," he observed.

"I told the colonel that you'd release his brother's body tomorrow."

"Why not today? I'm finished with it."

"I need another day."

"Why?"

She shook her head. "I'm not sure yet. Just play along for a day, huh?"

"Sure."

"Thanks."

"What do you have in mind, Sharyn?"

"I don't know. I'm still working on it."

He nodded. "Sure. I'll get the paperwork done on the Metzger case. *Slowly*. You finally agree that it wasn't an accident?"

"Yeah," she agreed. "I guess I do."

Sharyn took her place in her chair and gathered the papers together on her desk. She put Nick from her mind and concentrated on everything that they had learned about Tom Metzger's life. She looked closely at the mystery woman's face.

"Where are you?" she asked aloud. "Who are you?"

The woman stared mutely back at her. Was she the key?

What was she missing? Sharyn ruminated over the author's death. She checked the file. There had been no response to calls and enquiries about Joanna Powers. No one had seen a woman with the colonel at the hotel. There was no driver's license picture for Mrs. Metzger. Nothing to connect her to Tom Metzger. Nothing except her wedding announcement to connect John Metzger to Joanna Powers Metzger. *Joanna Metzger.*

J. M., written so often in Tom Metzger's planner, could be Joanna Metzger. Maybe the colonel's wife and the mystery woman were the same person.

Had the younger brother finally upstaged the elder, with the one woman who really mattered? If so, it might not be the mystery woman who rolled the truck down the ramp with the unconscious author at the wheel. But how would she prove it?

She was about to pick up the phone when Trudy

poked her head around the door and called her name. "Line two, Sheriff. Nick."

Sharyn picked up the phone. "Yes?"

"I need you to come down here right away, Sharyn."

"All right."

"Now," he added, then the line went dead.

She glanced at the clock. It was nearly 8:00 P.M. and she hadn't had dinner. She was exhausted and her head hurt. She rubbed her head with her hands and ran a hand through her tumbled mass of curls. Then she put on her hat and went out the door.

"Your mother called," Trudy told her. "She wants you to know she's going out with the senator tonight. She said not to wait up."

Sharyn grimaced. "I wouldn't think of it. Go home, Trudy. What would Commissioner Swindoll say about all this overtime?"

Trudy smiled. "He told me to stay and answer questions from reporters in such a way that he was all but the hero of solving the murder cases."

"Great," Sharyn declared. "Never mind him. Go home, Trudy."

"Yes, ma'am."

Ed was on his way out to work his double shift taking over David's patrol. Ernie and Joe were out trying to find out if Del Anderson had an alibi for Sunday night. Sharyn hitched a ride with him to the hospital since the other patrol cars were out.

"I talked to David," he told her. "He's a stubborn young mule."

"He doesn't want his job back?" she guessed.

"That's about the size of it. He's applying for a job at the college as a security guard. He says that anything would be better than working with you, Sheriff, begging your pardon."

"That's okay. I know I embarrassed him by calling him down about the investigation and his overall job performance since he started dating Regina."

"The girl has turned his life around and not in a good way," Ed said. "I don't know what to do with him. But if he doesn't come to his senses soon, I'm going to take him to the woodshed. His daddy might be dead but that doesn't mean he doesn't need a good whipping."

"Good luck," she wished him as he slowed the car to a stop at the hospital. "See you later, Ed. Thanks."

"Sure thing, Sheriff."

Sharyn yawned as she walked down the empty, dark corridors that led to the morgue. It was oppressive enough being there during the day. She didn't know how Nick worked there day and night.

"I found something," he told her when she walked in the door. "I was so swamped that I was letting my students go through some of the evidence. Someone missed something that might be important."

Sharyn nodded. "I know you need a permanent full-time assistant. I plan to ask the county about it next month."

"Swindoll will never go for it," he disagreed. "But thanks for trying."

"What is it?" she asked.

"I was going through Metzger's stuff, getting it ready to release, and I found this." He held up a plastic bag. "Cigar ash."

"Cigar . . . can we tell what kind?" she asked quickly.

"Do we know if he smoked?"

"Do we?" she asked him.

He shrugged. "I checked his body. There were no tobacco stains on his fingers or teeth. His lungs were clear. If he smoked, he was incredibly clean and he didn't inhale."

"There we go back to his being incredibly clean," she mentioned.

"Impossibly clean," he added. "He couldn't have totally disguised the fact that he smoked. Even if it had been for a short time."

"His brother smokes," Sharyn observed with narrowed eyes as she looked at the cigar ash.

"But the colonel didn't get up here until after his brother had disappeared," Nick related.

"He *said*." Sharyn nodded. "We couldn't confirm an exact time, just approximate. From the time we have him at a gas station in Virginia, it's close. Can we find out what kind of cigar it came from?"

"Sure. It will take a while. I'll have to send it to an expert. I'm not Sherlock Holmes."

"That's fine. In the meantime, I'll have a talk with Colonel Metzger."

"But not alone?" he pressed.

"You sound like Ernie," she told him. "I have to do my job."

"I could come with you," he volunteered. "You could call Ernie from here."

"This is something I need to do alone," she answered, a plan forming in her mind.

He looked down at the dull green floor. If the janitorial staff made it down there once a month, they were doing good.

"I'm sorry this happened. You were right. I was too intent on proving that Del did it, I guess."

"You were overworked and understaffed," she corrected him, picking up the telephone. "You did the best you could and it might be just as well that you wanted this investigated as a homicide."

"But we might not have the right man."

"All the better." She waited for her mother to answer the phone. "If the colonel is involved with this, he'll be thrown off guard by Del's arrest. He and Caison Talbot and Ty Swindoll were all patting each other on the back at the courthouse. I almost passed out from the horror of it."

He laughed as she told her mother that she needed a ride before she went out on her date. Her mother agreed to come and get her.

"Be careful," Nick warned when she had hung up the phone.

"I'm always careful," she replied, looking at him, wondering what he was thinking.

She took out her notebook and dialed the number for the hotel where the colonel was staying.

"Yes?" he answered in a clipped, angry voice.

"This is Sheriff Howard," she told him. "Sharyn."

"Sharyn." His voice changed. "What can I do for you?"

"Since the case is over and you haven't left town yet, why don't we go out for a few drinks and some dinner?" she suggested. "I can be ready in an hour."

"That sounds great," he replied. "What made you change your mind?"

"I told you," she answered saucily. "I didn't have any free time until the case was solved. Now that it's over, we can get together."

He laughed. "That sounds intriguing. I can't wait.

Wear something special for me, Sharyn, and don't be afraid."

"I wear my Grandad's gun, John. I'm always ready for danger."

She hung up and realized that Nick was listening intently to her conversation.

"Is that your idea of being careful?" he demanded, confronting her. "That man is a weirdo, Sharyn. Encouraging him isn't safe!"

"Not necessarily," she admitted, "but it might lead him to let his guard down enough for me to get the truth from him."

"You expect him to admit he killed his brother?"

"No," she said with a smile. "But cigar ashes aren't much to go on, even if we prove they're his brand. We need a motive. We need to understand what makes this man tick. We need a picture of his wife."

Nick shook his head. "You shouldn't do this alone."

"I think he might get suspicious if Ernie or Ed come with me for an intimate dinner, Nick. I'll be fine."

"Sharyn!" He put both of his hands on her shoulders. Their faces were very close, their eyes burning holes in each other's faces.

"Nick," she said quietly. "It's my job."

He looked at her a moment longer, then he dropped his hands to his sides. "All right. I'll send off the ashes tonight. I'll do *my* job. Just be careful. Don't take any chances."

She smiled. "I'll try to remember all of that. Anything else?"

He shook his head. "Call me when you find out anything."

"I will. Good night, Nick."

"Good night, Sharyn," he said calmly. He watched her walk out of the morgue and picked up the phone. "Find Ernie Watkins for me."

Chapter Ten

Sharyn went home with her mother. She refused to answer her mother's questions about where she was going or what she was doing. It was bad enough to have Nick feel that she couldn't handle the situation with the colonel. She didn't need her mother questioning her judgment.

Faye was used to her daughter keeping things from her. She chatted about Caison and their upcoming dinner. She talked about Kristie coming home the next weekend. She knew from Sharyn's tight-lipped, single-word responses that she wasn't listening.

"I don't like the way you look, Sharyn," she said finally. "You look very pale tonight. Can't you put off whatever you have planned until tomorrow?"

"No, Mom. Tomorrow may be too late. I'll be fine."

Faye patted her hair in the rearview mirror and swung the car to the right, causing a passing car to blow its horn at her.

"It's been my experience that anything can wait until the next day, Sharyn. I think you need to rest. Let someone else do whatever this is."

Sharyn closed her eyes in the late evening darkness. "I'll be fine."

Faye didn't argue the point. When Sharyn came out of her room, dressed in a pretty turquoise sundress, her mother took it all back. If Sharyn was dating, she would feel a lot better leaving her if she decided to marry Caison.

"You look wonderful, dear! Those earrings and the matching clip in your hair are just right. And that trace of sunburn colors your face wonderfully."

"Thanks," Sharyn said, slipping her feet into sandals. "I'll probably be out late. Don't wait up for me."

"We'll be late too, dear." Faye told her as Sharyn picked up her car keys from the hook by the door. "Sharyn? Are you sure you're all right?"

"I'm fine," she reassured her mother again. "Good night, Mom. I'll see you tomorrow."

Faye watched her daughter drive away in her shiny black Jeep. She sighed, thinking about her relationship with Sharyn. But she didn't know how to relate to a daughter who carried a gun and refused to have her nails manicured. The phone rang and she picked it up. It was Ernie.

"She's gone," Faye told him when he asked her if Sharyn was there. "Is something wrong?"

Ernie assured her that everything was fine. Faye knew by the tone in his voice that it wasn't true. Something was wrong.

Every time Sharyn went out, it was a reminder of the times she had waited for her husband to come home, always worried that he wouldn't come home at

all. Then he had been killed and her worst fears had
been realized. She could only pray history wouldn't
repeat itself with Sharyn. She picked up the phone
again and called Caison.

Sharyn arrived at the hotel around nine-thirty. There
was still a lot of traffic on the interstate and around
the hotel. The hotel bar and restaurant were full of
people. Loud music blared out into the darkness.

She smoothed down her dress with a shaking hand.
She'd seen actresses on television do this sort of thing
but she had never envisioned herself trying it. Her
style was more up front. But in this case, they had
very little time and an up-front approach would defeat
their advantage.

She carried a small revolver in her purse. There was
nothing else to get in the way of a quick retrieval. If
things turned ugly, she hoped that she was ready.

She didn't have a plan, exactly. It was more what
she could glean from the colonel since he knew that
the investigation was over and the culprit was sup-
posedly in jail. He would be relaxed and hopefully
distracted by thinking that she was interested in him.
She would be able to ferret out information about him
that would tell her if he had killed his brother.

It seemed unlikely. Maybe even wishful. Cigar
ashes could have come from anywhere, even if Tom
Metzger hadn't smoked. Yet instinct was guiding her
that night. She knew that she was on the right track.

She knocked at the door and the colonel answered.
His eyes glided over her appreciatively.

"Come in," he invited. "Nice dress. You look
great."

"Thanks," she replied, surprised by the lavish com-
pliment. She walked into the room and saw the table

set in front of the curtained window. There was a bottle of wine in a bucket of ice and two plates.

"Are we eating in?" she asked, turning back to him as the lights went dim and Frank Sinatra started singing in the background.

"I thought it might be more conducive," he answered smoothly, taking her purse from her and setting it on the dresser. "Dance?" He took her hand in his and pulled her to him.

John Metzger was a handsome man in a cold, hard way. His hand was firm on her spine as he moved with her across the limited floor space. He smiled down at her in a deliberate fashion.

"After all," he continued in a low growl, "we both know why you're here."

She didn't deny it. They both seemed to have an agenda. Even if it was a different agenda.

"I love this dress," he remarked again, his hand splayed out on her warm back. "You're so correct and well mannered on the outside, Sharyn. I'll bet you're a tiger on the inside with that red hair and those gorgeous lips."

"You're very attractive too," she responded lightly. "You're so strong and . . . and forceful, Colonel."

"Call me John," he said, sweeping her into a dip across his arm.

Sharyn forced herself not to struggle. She lay quiescent in his arms and smiled up at him.

"How about some wine?" he asked her. "Dinner will be here later. When we call them."

"That would be great, John," she added for substance. "I'd like to freshen up."

"Help yourself," he advised.

She heard him humming to the music, completely

at ease. She was disturbed that she had misjudged the man so badly. Ernie had been right. He was really interested in her. If it had been something to throw her off, he was still ready to go with it. Of course, what did he have to lose?

Quickly, she went through everything she could find in his bathroom. There were the usual toiletries, comb and brush. A pair of shoes sat under the sink, freshly polished. She looked inside the only drawer in the bathroom and found his razor, a straight edge, and a small mirror. There wasn't anything else.

She glanced at herself in the mirror over the sink. Her face was a little red but she looked normal otherwise. She was going to have to get him out of the room to search through his things. Her mind raced, trying to think of a way to do that without alerting him.

"Ready yet, angel baby?" he called.

She grimaced at herself in the mirror. "Coming."

Quickly, she kicked off her sandals by the bathroom door.

He looked down at her bare feet. "Well, I see you're comfortable."

She smiled, looking at him with questing eyes.

"Tonight!" He raised his glass to her. "To memories of this night together."

Sharyn remained silent, conscious of the way he might have killed his brother. He didn't have any reason to hurt her, she reminded herself. He trusted that she was there to have a good time.

"Shall we have another dance?" he asked her.

Sharyn put down her glass and walked up to him, acting as much like a femme fatale as she could imagine. She put a hand on the front of his shirt and felt his heart beating beneath her touch.

"How about going out dancing? I can be ready when you are," she whispered.

"Honey, I was born ready," he told her with a laugh.

"Let me get my purse," she said, walking to the dresser and looking inside the purse. "Oh, no!"

"What's wrong?' he asked at once.

"I left . . . something . . . in the car. I'll be right back."

He grinned. "You've got your shoes off already, let me get it for you."

She handed him her car keys. "Black Jeep. There's a package on the front seat. Thanks."

"I'll be back."

As soon as the door closed behind him, she was moving around the room. There was an ash from one of his cigars in the ashtray on the bedside table. She emptied it into a plastic bag she found on a water glass. She rummaged quickly through his drawers but there was nothing other than clothes in them.

There was duffle bag in the closet. She used another plastic bag to secure an empty bottle of sleeping pills and the packaging that went with it. There were gloves in the bag as well and some residue of white powder she was willing to bet was crushed sleeping pills. They would have to have the bag to analyze it.

She took a deep breath and opened his wallet that he had left lying on a bedside table. There were credit cards and a few hundred-dollar bills. There were receipts and his membership card to the NRA as well as his driver's license and his military ID. There was a picture—

The door opened and Sharyn closed the wallet and put it back on the table.

The colonel hadn't lost his amorous glow. He

handed her the package he'd found on the car seat and leered at her. "Miss me?"

Sharyn took the video box from him and smiled. "Maybe."

"Well, all that fresh air made me hungry. Let's order dinner."

She went into the bathroom and put the video box down, wondering how she was going to get out the way she came in.

When she came out she asked for a glass of water and looked down into it.

"Expecting to see something in there, sugar? Reading your tea leaves or . . ." He paused and his face changed. His eyes turned dark. "You know, don't you?"

"Know?" she faked.

He laughed, but it wasn't the carefree laughter from a few moments before. "Don't play games with me, *Sheriff*. You know. And you came here to check me out."

Sharyn realized that she wasn't going to get anywhere pretending with him. She faced him with a fixed expression.

"I know," she repeated. "It was your wife, wasn't it? For once, the tables were turned and your brother was taking your wife away from you. J. M. Joanna Metzger. It was all over your brother's planner."

He grinned. "Ironic, isn't it? That she would want him! Do you know how many women I took from him? And the pleasure I received doing it, I can't express. He was a pompous, arrogant, spineless idiot. And my wife was involved with him for a year before I found out about it!"

"You followed her here," she suggested, wondering

how she could get close to her purse on the opposite wall.

"I did. I was sick when I saw them together! I waited until she left and I took care of her. Then I talked him into going down to the site and I offered him coffee. He never knew what hit him. He was behind the wheel of the truck and in the lake and he never knew it!"

"That took something away from it, didn't it?" she asked, trying to keep him talking as she moved away from him.

"A little, but mostly he was dead and that was what was important. He told me about the plane in the lake and that the pilot's old girlfriend told him that she thought her beloved was killed. I knew I could use it to cover it all up."

"What do you mean, you took care of your wife?" she wondered aloud.

"What do you think, Sheriff Sharyn?" he mocked her slightly southern accent. "Want me to take you there?"

Sharyn shook her head. She was within arm's reach of her purse.

"So, now what am I gonna do with you?" he asked her, pressing closer as she backed away. "There's only so much room, you know. Eventually, you'll have your back against the wall."

He didn't wait for that moment. He lunged for her. Instinctively, she threw the glass of water in his face and followed it for good measure with the glass itself.

She dove for the purse but before she could get the gun, he was on top of her.

"Sheriff Sharyn, this is gonna be a big thrill for me. I have plans for you. I'm going to throw you into the lake. You'll be fish food."

"I swim," she told him through gritted teeth, trying to keep his hands from around her throat.

"Not with a rock around your neck, honey!"

His hands closed around her neck and they were squeezing. She was choking, tears streaming from her eyes. Her hand flailed out to search for anything to break his hold on her. It encountered something hard and cold. She picked it up and hit him as hard as she could. The vase broke, the glass shattering over both of them.

Col. John Metzger toppled to one side and Sharyn used the moment to gain leverage. She used the cord from her purse handle to tie his hands together behind his back, breathing hard as she leaned over him.

The hotel room door burst open and Nick, Ed, and Ernie stood in the doorway, guns drawn.

Sharyn looked at them, surprised.

"Are you all right?" Ernie asked, taking in the scene.

"I'm fine," she answered, showing him the broken vase. "He might need stitches."

"What about you?" Nick wondered, looking at her.

"I never felt better," she told him. "My headache finally went away."

Ed replaced her makeshift handcuffs with the real thing. The colonel was dazed. He groaned and tried to focus and found his hands cuffed behind him. He looked at Sharyn and uttered a foul epithet. Ed pushed his face down into the carpet with his boot. "I think it's time I take this mistake down to the jail."

"Don't forget Miranda," Sharyn reminded her deputy. "We don't want him to get away."

"Why did he do it?" Ernie asked.

"The mystery woman, J. M.," she explained

brightly. "She was his wife, Joanna Metzger." She showed them the picture of the mystery woman in his wallet. "He took all the other women away from his brother but Tom had his wife. He said he followed her here then killed her when she left. Then he took care of his brother."

"And he almost got away with it because of that first murder that Del confessed to!" Ernie said. "Del was ready to confess to Metzger's murder for the lighter sentence. Michaelson isn't going to like this."

She went to the closet and took out the duffle bag, giving it to Nick. "I think part of your mystery is in here. The empty sleeping-pill package. There's some residue that might be from him crushing the pills into the coffee and I pilfered a cigar ash from the table."

"You did it all, didn't you?" Nick asked cryptically. "No help from anyone."

She grinned. "Is that a bad thing?"

"Ever heard of teamwork, Sheriff?" he asked before he took the duffle bag and left the hotel room.

Ernie grimaced when she looked at him. "He was, uh, worried about you." He coughed and cleared his throat and looked at the floor.

Sharyn shrugged. "I'm going home to change and go to bed. Nick's people will take the room apart. Let's just make sure the hotel knows they can't touch it until then."

"You got it," Ernie answered. "Good job, Sheriff. You were right about Del."

"And Nick was wrong," Ed concluded. "That's probably what's sticking in his craw."

"See you both tomorrow. Thanks for coming to help."

Sharyn went home, showered, and fell into a deep

sleep. Her mother was out so she didn't have to explain what had happened. When she finally awakened the next day at 7:00 A.M., the morning paper carried the story.

"You went to the hotel room alone?" her mother demanded when Sharyn appeared in her uniform, ready for work.

"Thanks, Mom," Sharyn said with a frown. "When Kristie gets an award for twirling her baton at a football game, you're thrilled. I bring down a murderer and you lecture me. I'll see you later."

Faye shook her head and went back to her paper.

The office was in an uproar when Sharyn arrived at work. She waded through reporters to get into the building, ignoring questions as she went up the stairs.

"What's up?" she asked Trudy. "Did the colonel escape last night?"

"He's booked up tight and solid," Ernie told her, coming around the corner. "He even told Michaelson where to find his wife in exchange for some consideration during the trial."

"So, what's up?" Sharyn repeated her original question.

"There's a little boy missing from one of the new subdivisions outside of town. He and his family were up in the park on top of the mountain and he wandered away."

"How long?" Sharyn asked.

"They've been looking for about an hour. They camped up there last night, so they aren't sure how long he's been gone."

"How old is he?" she asked him.

"About three. Name's Jacob."

She nodded. "Have you called in the helicopter?"

"No," Ernie told her. "I wasn't sure if I should send it out. The money—"

Sharyn waved him away. "Call in the helicopter and let's get Doody Franklin and his hunting dogs. Does someone have a picture of Jacob? Have we asked for volunteers?"

Ernie produced a picture and Sharyn sent out to have copies made of it to distribute to the searchers. One group, worn to the bone and discouraged by not finding the little boy, returned to the office.

"Let's get a map going so we aren't searching the same areas over and over," she said to Joe.

He nodded and went to find a map.

Sharyn hitched a ride on the helicopter up the mountain. She used the map to coordinate the search from the areas that had already been searched. A team of volunteer firemen joined them and they walked the thickly forested mountain trails carefully, looking for Jacob's red jacket and blue cap.

There was some wildlife on the mountain. Deer and the occasional fox. Their most dangerous enemy was time. The longer the boy was out on his own, the better the chances he would fall off of a rocky ledge or be injured sliding down a muddy path.

Doody Franklin's dogs could be heard in the distance, barking as they searched for their quarry. They'd found more than one lost soul on Diamond Mountain. Sharyn hoped they would find Jacob.

By noon, the search was in full throttle. The helicopter flew close to the edge of the mountain, radioing what they found, while searchers on foot sent back their results. Nothing.

The sun was hot overhead, burning off the mountain mists. Ty Swindoll had come up the mountain to be involved in the search or at least the photo opportunity it presented. Caison Talbot followed closely on his heels.

Sharyn received a report from the helicopter that they were flying low over what was called the Diamond Back trail because of its twists and turns. Jacob's parents were huddled miserably together with friends who had gone out and come back again, exhausted and filthy.

"I see something." Word finally came back to Sharyn.

"What?" she asked quickly.

"Red jacket, blue cap, right?" the helicopter pilot confirmed.

"Is that him?" Jacob's mother stood up and ran to where Sharyn was perched on a picnic bench.

"Yeah. Have you got him?" Sharyn asked.

"Got him!" one of the four techs trained to fly the helicopter called back. "He's okay. I'm signaling the team I see a few hundred yards away. They should have him. I'll pick them up and we're on our way."

A wild cheer went up from the crowd that had gathered on the mountaintop. Jacob's parents were weeping and laughing as they hugged each other. Ty Swindoll took the initiative to speak with the press before anyone else could get there. He positioned himself in front of the television camera, tears streaming down his thin face.

"What can I say?" he shouted joyously. "The child is safe!"

Sharyn jumped down from the picnic table and joined him.

"Thanks to the emergency services department and the county's foresight to have a helicopter for times like these, Jacob Smith is coming home. It must be gratifying, Commissioner Swindoll, to know that you were instrumental in bringing the helicopter to Diamond Springs."

Swindoll looked at her. "Oh, yes! The helicopter and its pilots were very important in this search."

"But weren't you against the helicopter at the commission meeting last week, Commissioner?" Someone asked from the crowd of reporters.

"Against? Oh, no! You misunderstood me!"

"Didn't you threaten to fine the sheriff for using the helicopter last week?"

Ty smiled and put an arm around Sharyn. "We've settled that little misunderstanding, haven't we, Sheriff? The helicopter program is essential to this area."

"That's why the commissioner is going to vote for funding to train some new pilots in case of emergency," Sharyn prompted. "We only have a few pilots right now. Not enough for the real emergencies that can come up."

Swindoll nodded. "That's right. This is an important program. There's bound to be funding for this."

Sharyn shook the commissioner's hand while Swindoll's eyes shot sparks at her.

"Thank you, Commissioner.

"Thank you, Sheriff."

Sharyn turned away, feeling good that she had beaten Ty Swindoll at his own game. Now when she approached him for funding for a medical examiner assistant, what could he say? They had caught a killer because of Nick and his work. She knew she could shame him into providing the funds that they needed. The county was growing. The sheriff's department was going to have to keep up with that growth.

"Sheriff." David approached her as she walked away from Ty Swindoll's interviews.

Sharyn stopped and looked at him. He was filthy from hiking in the woods all day. Leaves and spider webs were stuck in his hair.

"Hi, David."

"It's great we found him and he's okay, huh?"

"Yeah, it's great," she agreed. "Have you been up here all day?"

"Yeah, since early this morning. As soon as I heard. I wanted to help. To be part of the effort."

She nodded. "You're a good man, David."

"I'm a better man now, Sheriff," he told her with a small smile.

"Better?" she wondered.

"Yeah." He glanced out at the mountain. "I gave up Regina. She was killing me."

Sharyn laughed. "I'm sorry."

"Thing is, I'd like to come back. To the office, I mean. I remembered what it was I liked about being a deputy. It was being part of it all. Helping out. Taking care of things."

She searched his face closely. "I haven't hired anyone to take your job, David. You're welcome back any time. Even with Regina."

They both laughed.

"Thanks, Sheriff. I'll be back tonight, if that's okay?"

"That's great. Tonight was my night for double duty!"

He smiled. "You don't mind if I try to take your place, do you, Sheriff? I've kind of always had a hankering to be sheriff."

"Not at all," she replied lightly. "As long as you do it in an election."

"You did a good job on the Metzger case," he told her. "You're a good sheriff." He smiled again. "Just that I'd be better."

Sharyn shook his hand. "Welcome back, David. Good luck."

"Sheriff." Ernie joined her. "There's a disturbance out at the Rokers' place. Hi, David."

David said hello and told Ernie he was coming back to the job.

"Good. That's good. We missed you."

"David's coming back tonight," Sharyn told him. "And now that things are quiet again, I'm going to take the last three days of my vacation."

"All right, Sheriff," Ernie said with a shrug.

"Don't send the helicopter for me, no matter what happens," she told him, climbing into her patrol car.

"No, ma'am."

"See you on Monday."

Sharyn was walking down the last of the Diamond Back trail. It was a grueling five-mile hike up and down the side of the mountain, through some dry creek beds and across part of the river that fed into Diamond Mountain Lake. She was exhausted, but she hadn't felt so good in weeks.

The day had been bright and clear. A late-night rain had kept the heat down and the mist that had swirled around beneath her feet was damp and cool. She pushed back her baseball cap as she moved around the last outcropping of rock, feeling with her hands along the rock face for the familiar holds dug into the rocks from countless hands before hers.

She stepped quickly around the six-inch ledge that dropped down a sheer fall to the lake below. Pebbles skittered down the side of the mountain, joining boulders that had dropped there from countless ages ago to just last year. In the summer, it was a dry wash but in the winter and spring, the mountain fed the lake with a cold stream you could reach down and drink from with your cupped hand.

Sharyn had hiked that trail with her father so many times. She could probably hike it blindfolded. She hadn't been there since he'd died and the memory of their last time together there was bittersweet. They always made camp on the rocky flat shelf that came after the drop. It was at least twenty-feet wide and thirty-feet long. It overlooked the lake and the lights of the town as the sun went down. Her father had told her ghost stories up there and they had discussed philosophy and life's secrets when she was older. Now it would be just her alone with the twilight.

She jumped the last few feet to the ledge and the aroma of cooking food assailed her from the mountain. It was summer, campers were everywhere. She just hoped if she had to share the shelf with someone that night, they wouldn't be annoying.

She stood up and followed the path to the shelf. Already, twilight was settling in on the rolling Uwharries. The lights from Diamond Springs would be coming on, one by one, until they were a jeweled necklace across the darkened landscape.

"You took your time getting here," a familiar voice greeted her.

"Nick?"

"Dinner," he told her as he finished putting out food on a small camping table. "Manicotti, wine, bread, and the best view in the county."

"What are you doing up here?" she asked in disbelief.

"Not hiking, I can tell you that," he replied. "If we were meant to hike, we would have been born with hiking boots."

"How did you get up here?"

He glanced up into the air.

"Not the helicopter! Please tell me you didn't bring the helicopter up here?"

He shrugged. "It was on an emergency run. I just dropped off here for the night. They're making another emergency run in the morning."

"What's the emergency?" she wondered.

He smiled. "I'm not sure, you know? They didn't tell me. Let's eat."

She still stood in the same place. "Why did you do this?" she asked curiously.

"I owed you something. You might have saved my life under the water that day."

"So you decided to make me dinner?"

"Or at least bring it up to the mountain."

She took off her backpack and set it carefully on the ground with her sleeping bag. "It smells wonderful." She sniffed appreciatively. "Thanks, Nick."

"Thank *you*," he replied in a deep voice. "You're an amazing woman, Sharyn. Sometimes I wish you were just a little less amazing."

She looked at him in the gathering dusk. His eyes were very dark and his face was all planes and angles in the first twinkling of starlight.

"Thanks, I think."

"So, let's eat. What do you do on a mountain in the dark when you're done eating?" he wondered.

"Tell ghost stories," she answered, breaking off a piece of bread.

"Ghost stories?"

She nodded. "I know a few that will turn your hair white."

He sat opposite her. "Unrequited love, ghosts doomed to wander the mountain forever?"

"Something like that," she replied as the lights came on in the town below them. *Her town.* "Something just like that."